Montezuma's Castle
and Other Weird Tales

OFTEN AT NIGHT HE SPOKE WITH FIERY ELOQUENCE

Montezuma's Castle
and Other Weird Tales

Charles B. Cory

LEONAUR

Montezuma's Castle and Other Weird Tales
by Charles B. Cory

Leonaur is an imprint of Oakpast Ltd

ISBN: 978-1-84677-693-9 (hardcover)
ISBN: 978-1-84677-694-6 (softcover)

http://www.leonaur.com

Publisher's Notes

The views expressed in this book are not necessarily
those of the publisher.

Contents

Montezuma's Castle

"No," said the curiosity dealer, "that mummy is not for sale. I had too big a job to get it."

"Tell me about it," I asked.

The curiosity dealer carefully closed and locked the case, and then meditatively rolled a cigarette.

"Well, it was this way: you see I was out after snakes and other natural history specimens. I had a special order from a chap in New York for three hundred snakes—he wanted some big rattlers. I think I sent him some that pleased him; anyhow he paid for them all right. I had a customer who wanted a rattlesnake with a very big rattle, and I fixed up a snake for him on this trip and sent it to him afterwards. It had one hundred and eighteen rattles! I glued a lot of rattles together, and by taking off the buttons it was pretty hard to see where they were joined. This rattle was more than a foot long.

"There was another Eastern chap wanted an ibex, which he said was found up in these mountains. It had light-coloured horns curved over at the tips like a chamois and striped legs and eyes that stuck out like an antelope. He had heard about the ibex and wanted a pair. I told him I had often killed them, but they were hard to get."

"What is an ibex?" I asked.

"I'll be hanged if I know," answered the collector. "But there are fellows in these mountains who say that there really are such animals, and if he wanted to have an ibex, and had to have an ibex, I might as well get him an ibex as anybody else, even if I had to make one.

"But to get back to my story. I had a big outfit on this trip and I expected to get a lot of curios one way and another, what with snakes and animals of various kinds, besides all the things that I might pick up in the way of baskets and Indian relics, which might prove saleable. My outfit consisted of two wagons, five horses, and I had a Mexican along to look after the teams and do the cooking.

"After being out some two weeks we found ourselves near what is called 'Montezuma's Castle,' up by the Verde. There are a lot of caves scattered about up there, supposed to have been made by the Cave Dwellers, and many of them had never been touched or examined.

"I had an offer of good money for a mummy, and had tried making them from the bodies of Indian children, but I never could get them to look real. The bones are not crumbly enough, and the rags which the real mummies are done up in are pretty difficult to imitate.

"I was mighty anxious to explore the big caves, so off we went to the place, and I tell you the old ruin they call 'Montezuma's Castle' is a dandy, and don't you forget it. The castle is built on a ledge high up on the side of a mountain which hangs over at the top. The only way to get up is by ladders or ropes, and it is mighty hard to get there even then.

"Right near there, on the face of the high cliff, there are a lot of fine old Cliff dwellings, and some of them are more than one hundred feet from the base. These cliffs are straight up and down, sometimes nearly smooth, but often with narrow broken ledges here and there on the face of the wall.

"One particular cave which seemed to be a rather large one was about fifty feet up, and immediately below it were two or three small ledges, which, after I had looked the place over, seemed to me to be sufficiently wide to hold a ladder; and I came to the conclusion that if I wished to explore one of these caves I had better try the one in question.

"In my outfit I had two large tents, nine by fourteen, and the poles of these tents, it seemed to me, would answer very well

THE CASTLE IS BUILT ON A LEDGE ON THE SIDE OF A MOUNTAIN

for ladders if I connected them by pieces of rope. It was not necessary to make the steps very near together, and by cutting notches in the poles and tying pieces of rope across I succeeded in making two very good ladders, one fourteen feet long, with the two top poles—one from each tent; and two small ladders, each about seven feet. I made these last from the four upright tent poles, there being two to each tent, as you know.

"The foot of the cliff was rough, and the first fifteen feet or so we could climb easily to a broad ledge, then there came a space between nine and ten feet in height, which was as smooth and perpendicular as a wall. Here my first ladder was put up. Two small ledges above this, some three feet apart, and a wider ledge four feet higher, allowed me to climb up, without the use of ladders, to another ledge.

"From here I ran another small ladder up to a ledge which was between two and three feet wide; from this ledge to the entrance of the cave was about twelve feet, and my fourteen-foot ladder answered finely, but the difficulty was, it had to stand so straight that it was rather ticklish business going up; one could not help feeling that a slip or a little backward jerk would topple it over into the valley below, and as from the ledge where it stood to the bottom was some forty feet, a tumble on to the rocks would prove most unpleasant.

"However, my Mexican, Antonio, held the ladder, and by very careful work I succeeded in reaching the mouth of the cave and crawling in. I had no sooner entered than I felt pretty sure it had never previously been visited by any one since the original inhabitants left it. The first thing I did was to take a stout piece of twine from my pocket and fasten the end of the ladder to a piece of rock. Then I felt easier.

"There were numerous bits of broken pottery scattered about and one nearly perfect specimen. Besides these there was a very interesting bit of stone carving. These things I gathered together and placed in a heap near the entrance. I then went back and, taking a small hatchet which I had brought with me, commenced to dig about in the floor and pretty soon found this little child mummy.

"By the time I had taken it out I was pretty thirsty and hot, as you may suppose. I was careful and did not hurry matters, and the cave was like an oven.

"Wrapping the little mummy carefully in a big handkerchief which I had tied round my neck, I untied the twine from the ladder, and lowered the bundle slowly down to Antonio, my Mexican, who was standing at the foot of the top ladder. It reached him safely, but while he was untying it I carelessly dropped the end of the string. I went back, however, and gathered up the other relics, intending to take some of them down with me and then come back for the rest if I could not manage them all the first time.

"While I was looking them over I heard a crash and the sound of tumbling stones, and looking out I saw that the ladder had fallen, and commenced to curse Antonio for his carelessness; but imagine my horror when I saw him throw down the bottom ladder and then run as fast as he could towards the camp. My first and only thought was to pay Antonio for his treachery. It was evidently his intention to leave me safely housed in a place from which I could never escape alive, and start off the proud owner of the two wagons, five horses, and various valuables which he believed my boxes to contain.

"My revolver was still in my belt, and hastily pulling it I commenced shooting at the running figure, now some sixty or seventy yards distant. The first bullet knocked up a cloud of dust about three feet to his right and a little ahead, the second was still worse, but at the third he turned sideways, staggered on several paces, and fell among some loose rocks in a way that must have been unpleasant. He tried to get up again, but I now had his range pretty well and hit him again with the sixth shot; after that he lay pretty quiet, although I thought I saw him move his arm once or twice. I reloaded, having plenty of cartridges in my belt, and began shooting at him again. This time I hit him three times out of six shots, and as he had not moved for some minutes I concluded that he was dead.

"Then I began to think over how I was going to get down.

I was very thirsty and it was tantalizing to see the water down in the valley sparkling in the sunlight. It looked very clear and refreshing.

"I thought and thought, and the more I thought the more hopeless it seemed to me to plan a way to get down alive. There was one ladder still standing,—the second one,—but there was a space of some thirty feet before I could reach it. I had absolutely nothing, not even a string, to aid me in getting down.

"There was no use hoping for help from any one, for the place was rarely visited, and it might be weeks before any person would discover that I was there. I was getting more thirsty all the time, and, at last, I hated to go to the mouth of the cave, hot as it was inside, because the sight of the water nearly drove me mad. I amused myself by occasionally taking a shot at Antonio. I had his range down pretty fine, now, and rarely missed him. It was getting late, and the sun had long since sunk out of sight. Above the mountains there was one tall peak which I could see up the canyon. It stood out in the sunlight bright and shining, even after the canyon had become quite dark.

"As the sun sank lower and lower the darkness crept gradually up until only the very top was left a shining point. For a few minutes it shone a fiery red and then the light was gone like a huge torch which flickers and goes out.

"Then the night noises commenced: the incessant, maddening croaking of the frogs and now and then an owl.

"Did you ever hear the frogs in Arizona?"

I responded in the affirmative.

"Well, then, you know something about what they sound like, and know they can give Eastern frogs cards and spades and beat them easy. But you don't know what they sound like when you are *really* thirsty!"

"Probably not," I answered.

"Well," continued the curiosity dealer, "I knew nothing could be done until morning, so I lay down and tried to sleep. I was very nervous and could not help fearing that in the night I might walk in my sleep or roll to the mouth of the cave and tumble out. I do not think I really slept at all, but lay in a half-dazed condition until it was light enough for me to see things in the canyon below.

"Strange to say, I was not hungry, although I had eaten nothing since the previous morning. My whole thoughts were concentrated on the one desire—something to drink! I thought and pondered, trying to think of some possible way to get down! At one time I thought seriously of jumping to the ledge below, but I knew that it would be impossible for me to stay on it even if my legs were not broken by the fall, and that to jump meant practically to commit suicide!

"At last a thought occurred to me that I might possibly make a rope out of my clothes. I had a large pocket-knife and a hatchet, and no sooner had the thought suggested itself than I commenced to undress. My canvas coat, shirt, and trousers and some thin underclothes constituted my entire wardrobe, and by carefully cutting them into strips wide enough to bear my weight, and yet narrow enough to give sufficient length, I succeeded in making a kind of a rope with which I hoped I could succeed in reaching the second ladder without broken bones!

"I could not work steadily, as it was impossible for me to avoid getting up and now and then walking about the cave. I suffered so with the heat and thirst, that the hope of escape alone kept me from going mad. At last the rope was done and tied together with various knots. It had a creepy sort of stretchy feeling when I pulled on it, but I had no alternative but to trust to it,—it was that or nothing, and nothing meant death from thirst in a very short time.

"I succeeded in fixing the hatchet firmly into and across a cleft in the rock where it was split, and it gave me something to tie the rope to which I was satisfied would hold my weight. I tied the end of the rope to the hatchet handle and threw the other end down, and was mighty glad to see that it reached within four or five feet of the middle ledge.

"I was stark naked excepting my shoes, and I tell you it was no easy task letting one's self down over the sharp edges of the rock. Every moment I expected one of the knots to give way, and I shall never forget the feeling which came over me as I swung myself clear of the ledge and hung swaying on that improvised rope which seemed to stretch and grow thin in a way which sent cold shivers running up and down my spine. It seemed a year before I reached the ledge. I went down pretty slow, sparing the rope as much as I could by supporting part of my weight by digging my toes into every little crack and crevice I could find, but I got there at last, and when I did, I sat down on the ledge and cried like a baby.

"Well, that is the story. Of course I got down the rest of the way all right, or I wouldn't be here; but I don't know as I would have done it if Antonio had pulled down the second ladder instead of the bottom one. He was evidently in too much of a hurry to do the job up right. After reaching the second ladder, it was no kind of a trick to slide it down and use it over again. The first thing I did when I got down was to run as fast as I could to the river and drink as much water as I dared, then I lay down in the water and enjoyed it. Talk about your Paradise Cocktails— they are not to be compared with that Verde River water which I tasted that day!"

"Antonio?"

"Oh, yes, he is there yet, I believe, although I have never been back since to see, and I hope I never will. My first experience among the Cliff Dwellers was all sufficient."

The Amateur Championship

1

A committee from the Phoenix Athletic Club and one from the Prescott Club had met, and after considerable discussion had arranged a match to decide the Amateur Championship of Arizona.

As the Phoenix and Prescott clubs were far and away the foremost athletic organizations in the Territory, the contest was looked forward to with a great interest, especially as an intense rivalry existed between the two cities.

"Let the contest be fair and square on both sides," said Smith, the chairman of the Phoenix committee. "Let each club send its best man, who is strictly an amateur, of course, and a member of the club, in good standing, and let the best man win."

"Them's my sentiments exactly," responded Johnson, the chairman of the Prescott committee. "Fair play and honours' to the best man, say I! I did think of sending a young fellow I know in our club who took some sparring lessons in 'Frisco last year, and is quite clever; he's a gunsmith by profession, but the trouble is he has been teaching the boys during his spare time when he could get away from the shop, and that makes him a professional, doesn't it?"

"It does," said Smith, "and I am glad to find you are as particular as I am in such matters; let me tell you, it is a pleasure to meet a man like yourself who tries to be fair and square, and to take no advantage of anybody. Let's take something."

During the next few days there were anxious meetings of

the committees in charge of the arrangements. A certain man well up in sporting matters went to 'Frisco as a committee of one, representing the Prescott Club, to hunt for talent; at the same time a brother of the chairman of the Phoenix committee, who kept a bar-room in Chicago, received a letter which caused considerable discussion between him and his partner, and several interviews with a certain short-haired, thick-set individual who frequented his place. The letter said:

> What I want is the best man you can get. Some one who is a sure winner, and can punch the stuffing out of this amateur duck from Prescott. Don't make a mistake, and do not spare money. Get a star, as the boys will bet all they have on him, and we do not want to take any chances.

The following week the chairman of the committee of the Phoenix organization received a letter from his brother in Chicago, which informed him that for two hundred dollars, and expenses, they had secured the services of a well-known professional, but one who had never been West, and who, they were sure, could "lick" anything which could be produced, professional or amateur, on the Pacific Coast. He had commenced training, and they could rest easy, and bet as much money as they wanted to.

Meanwhile the Prescott Club's representative had made a rich find in San Francisco, in the shape of an Australian professional who had just landed and was therefore not likely to be recognized. He had a record of numerous victories in his own country, and cheerfully undertook, for the sum of seventy-five dollars, "to knock the bloomin' head off any bloomin' duffer," anywhere near his own weight, that might be brought against him.

Things went along merrily, letters were exchanged between the chairman of the two committees reporting as to the progress of their representatives. The Prescott leader wrote:

> Our young man is doing very well, and I hope great things from him. Naturally we want to win, and have secured the best man of good amateur standing in our town to repre-

sent us. He is a drug clerk, and his mother objected pretty strongly at first, but she has been talked over. There will be a party of at least one hundred of us go down with him, and I hope you will have front seats reserved for us. Most of the boys feel inclined to wager a little on the success of our representative, but he himself does not feel very confident of the result. Upon my return I found quite a strong feeling in favour of having the young gunsmith represent us, but, after my conversation with you, could not for a moment countenance any such proceedings on our part.

Two nights following, the Prescott chairman read the following letter in answer to the one which he had sent:

To R. W. Johnson, Esq.
Chairman of the Committee
Prescott Athletic Club
Prescott
Arizona

Dear Sir: I am glad to hear that there is considerable interest taken in the forthcoming match. Boxing is a noble art, and this coming contest will no doubt help to boom both our clubs. There is a great interest taken here in the match, and I warn you our man is getting himself in the very best condition possible. He is nervous, of course, this being his first appearance in an affair of this kind. He is a clerk in a bank, who has lately been engaged by my friend Robinson, and therefore does not get as much time for exercise as perhaps would be wise, but Robinson is an enthusiastic sport, as you know, and has arranged to let him get off several hours each day. We look forward to a great contest, and I certainly feel that the winner may fully consider himself the Amateur Champion of the Territory. We shall take great satisfaction in reserving the one hundred seats you ask for. I think you will find all the money ready for you in the way of bets that you will want. Our population is made up a great deal, as you know, largely of miners and ranchers, and they are inclined to bet recklessly. I cannot close without congratulating the Prescott Athletic Club for the energy and enterprise they have shown in this matter. May the best man win!

Yours, etc.

J. Smith

2

There was a great crowd packed into the ring of the Phoenix Athletic Association on the evening of the contest. Seats were at a premium, and the fight had been the principal subject of conversation for days. The two principals had met and been introduced to one another, just before going to the scene of the contest. Both were dressed for the occasion, and I tell you they were sights! The bank clerk had on a collar so high that he could hardly turn his head, a high silk hat, long black frock-coat, and an immense white rose in his buttonhole.

The Prescott drug clerk was still more gorgeous. Besides a buttonhole bouquet and high collar, he sported an eye-glass, and smoked a cigarette while in the presence of his opponent.

"'Ow's yer bloomin' 'ealth?" remarked the drug clerk. "Hi 'opes as 'ow yer fit."

"Ah-h-h, go arn," answered the embryo financier, using only one side of his mouth, "don't try ter jolly me, yer sage-brush dude, or I'll give yer a poke right here."

Several members of the committee hastened to interfere, and put a stop to all further danger of trouble by hurrying the principals off to their dressing-rooms to prepare for the contest.

In the ante-room Smith hugged Robinson, and nearly wept with joy when they were alone.

"Did you take a good look at the stiff?" he gasped. "Why, our man will punch daylight out of him in two minutes after the gong sounds! Why, I say this is wrong—it is too easy; I really feel sorry for these Prescott chaps!"

Robinson chuckled and muttered something about "fools and their money being soon parted," and then the two worthies repaired to the ringside.

Smith was to be Master of the Ceremonies, and climbing upon the raised platform he crawled through the ropes, and after looking about him for a moment, raised his hands to enjoin silence.

"Gentlemen," he said, "I must beg you all to stop smoking. The contest which is to be held here to-night is to decide the Amateur Championship of the Territory of Arizona. Nothing is more calculated to incite among our younger men the love for athletic sports than such competitions, when conducted in a fair and sportsmanlike manner. I must beg of you not to allow yourselves to be biased towards indulging in any unseemly noise in case your favourite should be worsted. What we want is a fair field and no favouritism, and while we hope our boy will win, none of you, I am sure, would wish in any way to feel that either man was given any undue advantage. The men will fight with 3-oz. gloves, Marquis of Queensbury rules, three minutes to each round, with a minute's rest between. A man down to get up inside of ten seconds or be counted out. No hitting in the clinches. Many of you are acquainted with the gentlemen who are our representatives this evening, but for the benefit of those who are not I will introduce them."

Waving his hand towards the Prescott pugilist, he said:

"This is Alexander Harrington, amateur champion of the Prescott Athletic Club, who is, I may say, by profession a popular druggist in the town from which he comes. (Considerable applause.)

"And this," he continued, pointing to the man who represented the Phoenix Club, "is J. Francis Livingstone, a young man who has shown himself to be a good exponent of the noble art, and who is deemed to be the amateur champion of the Phoenix Athletic Association. As he has only lately arrived, and is not very well known to many of you, I may add that he is a personal friend of our Vice-president, Mr. Robinson, and is employed at his bank. (Wild enthusiasm.) As there can be no question as to the amateur standing of the gentlemen, I will again beg of you to treat both men with equal favour, and will ask the Referee to call time!"

The seconds at this climbed down from the ringside, shoving their stools out under the ropes, and the two athletes, throwing aside their bath robes, stood up in their corners, each stripped to the buff, with the exception of tight trunks and canvas shoes. A roar of admiration and astonishment went up as the bank clerk first exposed himself, and Robinson grinned at Smith across the ring as the splendid exhibition of muscle was exhibited. It was evident that the bank clerk had not devoted all his time to banking; he was apparently as fit as a race-horse, and the muscles of his back and arms twisted and rolled about like snakes, at every movement.

But Robinson's expression altered somewhat as he glanced at the drug clerk. That individual was somewhat shorter than his opponent, but if the banking representative was well developed, he of the pharmaceutical persuasion was magnificent.

Both men had been fanned and washed, their gloves carefully tied on, and they now stood rubbing their shoes on some powdered rosin which was scattered about the corners, eyeing each other intently. What they thought will probably never be given to the public, but there is no doubt that each must have experienced a feeling of surprise at the physical condition of his opponent. This did not affect them in the least, however, as they were both as anxious to begin as bull-dogs, and when time was called and the gong rang, they danced to the middle and commenced sparring for an opening, grinning with confidence.

For the first minute or two nothing was done. Forward and back they moved, their arms moving in and out, each with his eyes fixed on the face of his opponent, watching closely for an opening. Then the bank clerk jumped in and led one, two, without effect, for his first blow was neatly guarded and the second brought a vicious cross-counter in return, which grazed his nose as he got back out of the way. In came the drug clerk with a rush, and they closed just as the gong sounded which ended the round.

Up through the ropes came the seconds with the activity of a lot of monkeys, and the two men were hurriedly seated upon stools and each was fanned furiously with a towel by one second, while the other bathed his neck and face with cold water. A hum of conversation arose.

"Who is the blooming duck?" whispered the druggist to his principal second. "'E ain't no bleeding dude, I can tell yer."

But before the man had time to reply, the gong sounded the call of "time," and the men sprang forward to the middle of the ring.

There was no sparring this time—they went at it biff, bang, right and left, sending in their blows with all the power of their muscular bodies. The Referee, almost dancing with excitement, shouted to them to "break away," and tried to part them when they clinched, but they were no sooner separated than they closed again, fighting with the energy and tenacity of bull-dogs.

Just before time was up, the drug clerk swung his right and caught the gentleman of finance fair and square on the nose, with the result that Prescott was awarded first blood and first knock-down, amid great excitement.

During the one minute's rest the seconds did wonders. The men were sponged and rubbed, while fanned constantly with a large towel, water was squirted on their heads and the back of their necks, and at the sound of the gong each arose from his stool looking as fresh as at the start.

Round 3 opened as though it would be a repetition of the hurricane style of fighting of the previous round, but after a clinch or two and giving and receiving a few good blows, the men kept apart and fought more warily. Each had evidently become satisfied that the other was not quite the easy victim he had expected; and as this conviction gradually dawned upon them they dropped the rough and tumble style and fought with more skill and caution, each watching and waiting for an opening, hoping for a chance for a "knock-out," but none came, and the round closed with honours even.

During the intermission Watkins, the sheriff, who was acting as Referee, talked earnestly with a friend, and from time to time looked hard at the drug clerk. He turned towards the timekeeper and seemed about to say something, when the bell rang and the men were again in the middle of the ring.

Round 4 had commenced.

They were both fresh and eager, but business was written all over their hard faces,—they were not smiling now. Round and round they moved, constantly facing each other, their arms moving back and forth like a machine. Now and then one or the other would make a quick feint or move, and the other would spring back with the agility of a dancing-master.

Suddenly the financier thought he saw an opening, and let go his left, but was short, and received a counter in return which sounded all over the place; then they went at it hammer and tongs and kept the Referee very busy separating them, and making them fight fair. Questionable prize-ring methods were resorted to by both men, and the knowledge shown by these amateurs of the little unfair tricks of the professional prize-fighter was astonishing. The bank clerk took especial pains to stick his thumb in his opponent's eye whenever they clinched, and the compounder of drugs used his head and elbow in a way which is frowned upon by advocates of fair play.

The men were fighting hard and fast when the round ended. Every man in the crowd was on his feet yelling like a hyena, as they went to their corners. Referee Watkins walked to the side of the ring, and raising his hand to enjoin silence, stood waiting for the uproar to subside. At last, when he could be heard, he addressed the crowd as follows:

"Gentlemen, I am sorry to stop this fight, but I must do it. These men are supposed to be fightin' for the Amatoor Champeenship of the Territory. Whether this is a put-up job or not, I do not know, but I do know that the Prescott man is a professional pug, lately arrived from Australia. I suspected him from the first. From the way he acted I was pretty blamed sure he was no drug clerk and my friend here, Jim Sweeney, swears he knows him, and that he was called the 'Ballarat Boy' when he saw him fight in Australia, some seven months ago. I can't let this thing go on, and have honest men lose their money. I am not dead sure in my mind that the other man isn't a ringer; he is a damned sight too good for an amatoor; but that cuts no ice. This fight stops right now. It's a draw, and all bets are off."

There was a tremendous row, but the pugilists were hurried off to their respective dressing-rooms, and the crowd slowly left the building. On the steps outside, Johnson, the chairman of the Prescott Athletic Club, met Smith, and, going up to him, he offered him his hand.

"Smith," said he, "I want to tell you how pained I am that the affair ended as it did. You, of course, do not for a moment suspect that any of us knew our man was a professional. How he could deceive us I cannot understand. Why, I was never more fooled in my life!"

Smith shook hands heartily. "Don't say a word, Johnson; the best of us are often deceived, and the more pure our motives are the easier it is to fool us."

"That's so."

They walked on in silence for a short distance.

"Smith."

"Hallo."

"Pity they stopped it; it was a lovely scrap while it lasted."

"That's what it was," said Smith.

The Tragedy of the White Tanks

"I do not believe," said the curiosity dealer, "that the bite of the gila monster is fatal. It is poisonous, no doubt, and there have been one or two cases of death where persons have been bitten by it, but it is always well to remember that the teeth themselves may be in a condition to produce blood-poisoning, which might cause death without the assistance of any particular toxic venom. The rattlesnake, however, which is rather too common in the desert, is a different sort of a chap. If he strikes you, you may just as well make your will, and chirp your death song, as to monkey with physicians, and squander some of the good wealth which may be useful to your family."

I asked him if he did not believe in the efficacy of some of the so-called Indian snake cures.

"There are lots of Indian remedies," he continued, "and snake charmers' cures for rattlesnake bites, which are, in my opinion, all poppy-cock. It is claimed that the Moquai Indians, during their Snake Dance, allow rattlesnakes to bite them, and after applying the juice of a certain herb suffer no ill effects from the poison. This may be all right, but the antidote is considerable of a secret, and you cannot buy it at your druggist's.

"There was a chap over in France who claimed to have produced an anti-venomous serum which was a sure cure for the poison of a rattlesnake, or any other old snake which you might want to have bite you. I squandered five dollars of my hard-earned wealth in sending for a bottle. This chap lives at Lille, France, and manufactures his serum at the Pasteur Institute at that place. He gives careful directions as to how much to use, and just how to use it, and it may be all right with some snakes which have the reputation of being bad, but it don't go with our rattlers. I tried it in all sorts of ways. I tried to get a Mexican to experiment on, but couldn't. None of them had much faith in the cure—not enough to let a healthy snake bite 'em for five dollars.

"Then I tried dogs. I got three curs, all in robust health. The first one died in fifteen minutes after being struck by a big rattlesnake which I had in a box, although I injected him with a carefully measured dose of the serum. Another one lived several hours, and made a hard struggle. I thought at one time he might pull through, but it was no use. He joined his friend in dog heaven after giving his final kick four hours and fifteen minutes after he and the snake had been introduced to each other.

"The third one was a half-breed bull bitch with lots of vitality. I tried to make this one immune by injecting a dose of the serum twenty-four hours before, and again immediately after she was struck by the snake, but she did not do as well as the other one, and died in three hours and sixteen minutes. All these dogs seemed to die from inability to breathe. The poison apparently acts on the respiratory centres rather than directly on the heart. They all vomited just before they died."

"Have you never found out what the Indians use as an antidote?" I asked.

"No, I have tried, but they keep it a carefully guarded secret. One reason why I believe that the secret is so carefully preserved is because they have no antidote, and the whole thing is a bluff.

"You see," continued the collector, "in my wanderings about the country I have run across a great many queer people, and as you seem interested in this subject, I will tell you an incident which happened while I was out at camp one time at the White Tanks, catching gila monsters, horned toads, etc.

"I remember the year well, because I had a lot of trouble with a very useless assistant of mine, whom I sent to Central America to collect for me. Among the birds he brought back were a lot of skins of the blue chatterer—the one with the purple throat, you know. He knew I was anxious to get new species, so he thought

25

he would be smart and make some for me. So he manufactured five, all with faked labels on, showing that each species was taken at different altitudes. Unfortunately he commenced too high, and the mountains in the vicinity where he collected, and where the labels indicated that the birds were taken, lacked several hundred feet of the necessary altitude for two of the species, so that if his labels were correct he must have shot them out of a balloon.

"They all looked alike except about the throat and head. One lot had a gold band across the breast, another had the whole throat gold, others had gold stripes or spots. I believe he produced these gaudy effects with the lighted end of his cigar.

"He doctored up a lot of humming-birds, too, and made me a peck of trouble. I fired him, all right. Dishonesty in a trade like mine is, I think, most reprehensible, and there is no money in it, because you are dead sure to get found out.

"He was a cute little chap, however, and had learned a lot of tricks from the Indians. He could change a bird's colour by feeding it on certain kinds of food. There is a chap in Amsterdam who does about the same thing and brightens up old worn birds which have faded out in the Zoological Gardens, and sends them back with all the brilliancy of their original plumage restored; but he cannot turn a red parrot blue, or make a gray bird with a yellow head turn to bright orange all over, as this chap could. He told me how he did it, but the secret is too good to give away. But to get back to the story about rattlesnakes:

"It was, as I said, in the spring of '89, a party of us were camped at the White Tanks about forty-five miles north-west of here, and one day a chap came into our camp, a half-breed Mexican Indian, who called himself a snake-charmer. He had a box of rattlesnakes which he would allow to twine round his neck and bite him, for a dollar. He travelled about the country giving exhibitions with his snakes, and selling the rattlesnake cure, which was put up in small bottles containing a brown-coloured liquid, which he claimed he made from a plant which was a sure cure for the bite of the rattlesnake, and a number of the boys bought this remedy, paying him a dollar a bottle.

"He had seen our camp, as he drove along the road to Phoenix, and he told us he had been up country for two or three weeks visiting some mines, where he had done very well, selling his cure to the miners and exhibiting his snakes.

"There were several of us in the party, and one chap, a doctor by the name of Baker, who was always playing practical jokes. As we were coming back to Phoenix, the next day, Miguel, which was the snake-charmer's real name, I believe, although he was generally known as Mexican John, decided to stay over a day and go back with us.

"Baker proposed that we should see how much faith Miguel had in his own antidote. As it happened, I had captured a very big rattlesnake the day previous, and had him in a box in my tent. By the aid of some forked sticks and bagging we succeeded in fastening the snake so that he could not move. We then pried his mouth open, and kept it open with a small stick. We took all this trouble for the purpose of preparing him to assist in an experiment in which he and Mexican John were to be the principal performers. Baker carefully cut out the poison-sacs, which are situated just beneath the temporal muscle, back of the eye. It was suggested that it would be better to remove the fangs, to avoid any possibility of danger; but Baker objected, as he said removing the fangs would give the whole thing away.

"He took the precaution, however, while the snake lay helpless with its mouth open, to carefully wash the teeth, and then filled the small openings near the end of the fangs with some dental cement which Baker had in his outfit, which hardens in a few minutes. You see, the fangs of a rattlesnake are like two hypodermic syringes. They are hollow tubes, as it were, with an opening near the point,—a little narrow slit, but one that is easily seen, if you look for it. Through this he squirts the poison by the aid of the temporal muscle, which he contracts as he strikes.

"As we had removed the poison-sacs and plugged up the fangs, this snake was not in a very good condition to do any serious harm. He, however, was fighting mad, and evidently did not enjoy the operation which he had undergone. It did not seem to hurt him any, however, for he was as lively as a kitten when we let him loose in the box, and was ready and anxious to strike at anything.

"Towards evening Miguel came back to camp, and we had the snake all ready for him. It was a much larger one than those which he had in his box, and when we slipped it in among the others we could easily recognize it from its size. The boys asked John to give an exhibition of the curative powers of his snake cure, saying that they would like to buy some more, but wished to see it tried before doing so.

"John was quite ready, and after opening a bottle of the antidote he lifted the cover of his snake box, and reached in his hand to take one of them out. As he did so, he was immediately struck good and hard by our latest addition to the collection.

"My, how he carried on! He looked hastily into the box, and then at the marks on his hand, where the fangs had cut in. He gave one screech, grabbed a knife, cut the place wide open, and commenced to suck it fiercely, at the same time praying and cursing almost in the same breath.

"The boys begged him to apply his antidote, asking him what was the matter and why he appeared to be so frightened, but all the answer they could get was, 'Don't touch me. I am going to die! I'm going to die!'

"And say, what do you think? He *did* die! He got weaker and weaker. His teeth were clenched, and he refused to take whiskey, although the boys forced some down his throat. In a little while he became insensible, and in less than an hour he was dead.

"'Scared to death,' you say? Well, maybe so; anyway, the boys said the laugh was on Baker!"

Too Close For Comfort

When Dr. Watson entered I saw by his manner that he had something of more than usual interest to communicate. Watson has a trick of winding and unwinding his watch chain around his finger whenever he has some case in which he is particularly interested. As a rule, his work in the asylum keeps him busy the greater part of the day, and the little time he has to spare is given to cases in which he is called in consultation or by special appointment.

Therefore, knowing how busy he was, I felt certain that something out of the ordinary had called him from his regular duties at this time of day, and I was interested to learn what it was.

Watson is nothing if not direct, and rarely wastes words. On this occasion he certainly lived up to his reputation, for he began talking before he was fairly in the room.

"My dear Morris," he said, "I have called to talk with you of a most interesting case, which has lately come under my observation. It is one in which I need your help, and I hope you will be able to spare the time to assist me."

I nodded and waved him to a chair.

"The case in question is a most interesting one, in which hypnotic suggestion may or may not be an important factor.

"You know young Blake, the son of the late Mathew Blake, and you are aware that he has been rather extravagant in his habits and ways of living, and although not exactly a spendthrift, undoubtedly spends more money than he ought to in many ways. The great trouble with him is his passion for race-horses, and that is what, one of these days, is going to break him financially, unless I am very much mistaken.

"Just now young Blake has two horses entered in the big race which comes off day after to-morrow at Eaton Park. One of his horses, called Emperor, is well known, and he should easily win the race. He is by far the best horse of the lot, and has been selling in the pools for two to one against the field. The other horse is not nearly as good as Emperor, and has little chance of being placed. Murphy, the jockey who is to ride Emperor, is one of the best on the turf, although comparatively a young boy, probably about nineteen years old. He has ridden a number of races, and from all reports is a lad of good habits, and seemingly thoroughly honest.

"Young Blake, as you know, 'plunges' more or less on his horses when they run, whenever he thinks they have a fair show to win, and in this case he has bet a great deal more money than he can afford to lose, knowing that unless the horse meets with some unforeseen accident he is certain to win the race. As I understand it, he has bet so much money that if by any chance Emperor should lose the race it would seriously hurt young Blake. Of course, this is all foolishness from our standpoint, but the fact remains that the young man has bet this money, and that any accident which would interfere with his pulling off that race would cause him serious loss.

"Knowing his father as I did, I have taken more or less interest in the boy, and have time and again advised him to let racing alone, and settle down to more serious life. I should not have taken the special interest in this particular race had it not been that by a curious coincidence information has come to me which leads me to suspect that everything is not as it should be at young Blake's stables.

"Last year one of the stable boys, a lad by the name of Collins, was badly injured by an accident, and young Blake saw that he was nicely taken care of, and paid him a salary during his illness. The youngster was grateful, and the other day, it seems, he came to Mr. Blake and told him that Murphy, the jockey who is to ride Emperor, had been sleeping badly for several nights, and talked a good deal in his sleep about the horses.

"Murphy and Collins sleep together in the room over the stable, and the night before last Collins was awakened by hearing Murphy call out to some one, and then say distinctly, 'Yes, yes, I understand; if you wave your handkerchief I am to 'pull' Emperor. If you do not wave it I am to win, if I can.'

"This is serious business. The boy was dreaming, of course; but why did he dream such a dream? The idea of 'pulling' being in the boy's mind is in itself enough to cause serious reflection. Yesterday young Blake called on me and told me this story as it had been told to him by Collins. Collins was present at the time, and again repeated his statement, declaring positively that he could not have been mistaken in the words spoken by Murphy in his sleep, and that the boy seemed very much excited.

"Blake, by my advice, sent for Murphy and we had a serious conversation with him. The boy seemed thoroughly honest, and was very much hurt upon being questioned in regard to the matter. He said that he had worked for Blake several years and had always tried to do right, that he intended to ride his best, and win the race if he could.

"Blake naturally feels somewhat disturbed under the circumstances, but he believes the boy is honest, and he believes young Collins must in some way have been mistaken in what he imagines he heard. Or, if he was not mistaken, that Murphy was dreaming, and the words had no significance.

"He told Murphy to go back to the stables, and that he would trust him implicitly, stating at the same time that it would cause him serious inconvenience if by any chance Murphy should not win, as he had bet a large amount of money on the result.

"Murphy, with tears in his eyes, thanked him for trusting him, and went back to the stables. Afterwards I had a serious conversation with Collins, and learned that on two occasions he had seen Murphy talking with a strange man who often visited the track.

"Upon inquiry we have learned that the man in question is a brother of a man who married Murphy's sister, and that Murphy has met him several times at his sister's house. The man's name is Simms. He is a low character, who is known as a habitual frequenter of the race track, and who at times does business as a pool seller and bookmaker. Simms is described as being thin and dark, with a big scar on his right cheek, usually wears a soft hat, and carries a cane with considerable silver about the handle.

"Last night I decided to have an interview with Murphy and find out whether the lad could be hypnotized or not. Why this idea suggested itself to me I do not know, except that, as you know, hypnotism is one of my hobbies. With Blake's consent I sent for Murphy, and asked him to let me look him over, as I would like to assure Blake as to his physical condition, as naturally he was feeling, as I told him, somewhat nervous after our interview of the morning.

"The boy consented readily enough, and after listening to his heart, and asking him a few questions which might suggest a cause for his restlessness at night, I asked him to look at me fixedly while I gently stroked his forehead above the eyes with my hand. Imagine my surprise when I found him to be an extremely sensitive hypnotic subject. He did not become entirely unconscious, but was in a peculiar somnambulistic condition, in which he conversed readily enough. He is one of the best subjects for post-hypnotic suggestion that I have ever seen.

"I tried several experiments with him, and the thought occurred to me if it was not possible that this susceptibility to hypnotic suggestion might be used by unscrupulous persons in many ways, which might be especially dangerous in case he was riding a good horse in a race.

"Upon questioning Murphy, after I had awakened him, regarding his susceptibility to hypnotic influence, he told me that *Simms had often put him to sleep for fun, when they met at his sister's house.* The question which now presents itself is, Suppose he has been hypnotized and has been given a post-hypnotic suggestion, that he is to 'pull' Emperor if a certain man waves his handkerchief, how are we to prevent his carrying out these instructions? Of course, we can take the boy off the horse and put on another jockey, but Blake does not wish to do this.

"In his waking moments Murphy does not remember anything that has been told him while hypnotized, and I doubt if we could make Blake believe that there was any real danger in that quarter. Again, if we allow him to go in and ride the race, it is more than possible that he could be made to win or lose the race by any one who had given him orders while in a hypnotic condition, and we also know that he would forget entirely that he had received such orders after waking.

"Now, the difficulty presents itself as to how we can prevent him following out such instructions, in case he has received them. We know we cannot affect such suggestions by re-hypnotizing him, because we do not know the exact circumstances under which such directions were given. To merely hypnotize and tell him he is not to carry out such orders would have no effect whatever. Perhaps if we could tell him that under certain described circumstances he was not to carry out such orders we might succeed.

"But my experience has been that the directions, as given, are carried out by the subject if, at the time, the circumstance described, which is to be recognized as a signal for such and such action on the part of the hypnotized sensitive, occurs *and is noticed.*

"For instance, if I should hypnotize a young man, and say that at eight o'clock, when he hears the clock strike, he should at once go downstairs and get a glass of water, he would undoubtedly do it when the clock struck eight. But if the clock did not strike eight, supposing some one had removed the striker, and when near the hour some one occupied his attention so that he did not notice the time, in all probability he would not obey orders. It requires some special occurrence which has been described in connection with the act to suggest it again to his mind.

"In my opinion, the best we can do is to let Murphy ride the race, and to take all precautions possible to prevent any man waving his handkerchief to Murphy during the race. Of course, to have any real effect on the race, the person waving his handkerchief as a signal for Murphy to 'pull' Emperor must do so far enough from the home stretch to make it certain that Emperor can be prevented from winning without attracting especial attention, which could not be done in case Emperor was in the lead if the signal was given close to the Grand Stand. We, therefore, must look out for our man, if such a man there be, some distance down the race-track.

"Now, if you will go to the track with me to-morrow we will station ourselves in places where we think it likely that such a person would stand, and keep a sharp watch for a thin, dark man with a scar on his cheek. Will you join me?"

I assured him I would be more than willing to do so, as I was very much interested in the case.

"Good! Now, this is my plan. I shall take Mike Falan with me, and he is worth half a dozen men in the case of a row. I have also engaged three private detectives to be on the watch at the entrance to the Grand Stand, and another at the entrance to the grounds, while a fifth is to station himself at the side of the track, and do sentinel duty about the half-mile post, with orders to report to me the moment Simms puts in an appearance, and to have him shadowed. Of course, this elaborate plot may exist only in my imagination, but if, as I believe, there is a carefully arranged scheme to beat Blake's horse, we shall have done him a good turn, and perhaps saved him a lot of money. I must go now, but don't fail to meet me to-morrow at eleven, at the track. You will find me in front of the Grand Stand."

The next morning when I arrived at the track I found Dr. Watson in conversation with a powerful-looking man whom he introduced to me as Mike Falan. We walked slowly up the track to a point about a quarter of a mile from the finish. There was a great crowd of people present, the numbers had gone up for the first race, and most of the horses were already out and "warming up." Emperor appeared to be in splendid condition. As he galloped easily up and down in front of the Grand Stand his great muscles rolled and swelled under the shiny skin, and he looked and acted like a horse fit to race for his life. He was a prime favourite at the pools and was selling at two to one against the field.

"I have seen Blake," said Watson, "and he is feeling confident that Emperor will win. He is somewhat nervous, of course, but he tells me the horse is in first-class shape, and that Murphy is all right. No signs of Simms yet and the race will be started in less than ten minutes. It begins to look as though I have been frightened at a shadow."

At this moment a man touched Watson on the arm and whispered something to him and then moved quickly away through the crowd. Watson started, and turning to me said,

"Come this way. Simms is here, he is down the track, below the gate."

He hurried away, Mike and I following, and upon getting clear of the crowd we saw a man leaning against the picket fence which separated the track from the carriage drive, watching the horses through a small field-glass. As we came up, Simms, for it was he, glanced suspiciously at us, but as we paid no attention to him and talked earnestly together, apparently arguing as to the relative merits of the horses, he soon ceased to notice us and turned again to the horses.

Hardly had he done so when he hurriedly put the glass in his pocket, and a great shout from the Grand Stand and cries of "They're off!" told us that the great race had commenced.

We could see the horses far off on the opposite side of the track all running in a bunch, until they neared the half-mile flag, when two were seen to be well in advance of the others. As they swung round the curve we could see the red cap worn by Murphy flashing in the sun, and we knew that Emperor was leading. But another horse, a deep bay, the jockey dressed completely in blue, was very close to him.

On they came, and Watson and Mike edged closer and closer to Simms, whose whole attention was fixed on the race. His face was flushed, and he was actually dancing with excitement. We watched him as a cat watches a mouse, and it was very lucky for Blake that we did so. The horses were now quite near us, and we could see Murphy plainly, and noted how white and drawn his face looked. Suddenly Simms pulled a large white handkerchief from his pocket, but as he did so the doctor snatched it from his hand and at the same instant Mike seized him in his powerful arms, and dragged him from the fence.

Mad with surprise and rage, he struggled and kicked like a wild animal. "Damn you," he yelled, "let me go; let go, I say! What in hell do you mean?"

"Let him go, Mike," said the doctor. Mike pushed Simms from him, and he staggered back against the fence. The man was crazy with rage, and I believe for the moment he was really insane. He half crouched as if to spring at us, snarling and showing his teeth like a savage dog, then his hand went to his hip pocket.

"I wouldn't try that if I were you, Simms," said Watson quietly. "You will get the worst of it if you do."

Watson's right hand was in the pocket of his sack-coat, and his eyes said, "I'll shoot," as plainly as if he had told Simms so in so many words.

"See here, you," cried Mike, "if you pull a gun I'll smash your jaw!"

Simms looked from one to the other of us, with the expression of a madman. His face was ghastly white, and the scar on his cheek stood out livid, in contrast with the white skin. I thought for a moment he was about to draw his revolver, but suddenly he turned and ran toward the crowd, and in a moment was lost to our view.

The shouting and cheering still kept up, and, as we hurried toward the Grand Stand, Watson asked a man which horse had won.

"Emperor, by a length,—a great race!"

We found Blake in front of the stand. He came to us and shook hands. His face was beaming with the joy of success.

"Do you know," he said, "I do believe that something is the matter with Murphy. He was as pale as a ghost after the race. He said he could remember nothing about it until he found himself in the home stretch running neck and neck with Nettie B. Then he seemed to wake from a dream, and sat down and rode Emperor for all he was worth. You know the rest. He won out all right, but I tell you it was a confounded sight too close for comfort."

The Strange Powder of the Jou Jou Priests

Dr. Watson carefully opened the little antique silver box, which was about the size and shape of an ordinary watch, and showed that it contained a gray powder and a little gold measure resembling a miniature thimble. It was evidently very old, the cover being worn smooth in many places, nearly effacing the peculiar hieroglyphics with which it had once been engraved.

"I consider this," he said, "my *chef-d'oeuvre*, my 'star exhibit,' as it were. The powder possesses such wonderful properties, and is so unlike any known drug, that I hesitate to describe its effects. That it is a powerful poison there can be no doubt, but when taken in small doses it is apparently harmless enough."

"What is its history?" asked Dr. Farrington.

"I picked it up in London. Got it from Burridge, the explorer, who had just returned from a year's trip in the interior of West Africa. He went into Benin City with the English when they cleaned out the town. Burridge says he took it from a dead Jou Jou priest, and he made me pay a pretty stiff price for it. It is a wonderful drug, entirely unknown outside of Africa. Burridge thinks it is made from the leaves of some plant; but its preparation is a secret of the priests of Jou Jou.

"Now, I propose that we each take a small quantity of the powder to-night, and then dine together to-morrow evening and compare notes. I may as well tell you now, it produces strange hallucinations. I tried it once myself, and my experience on that occasion was, to say the least, peculiar; therefore I am more than anxious to try it again, and compare notes with you afterwards, and I think I can promise you a new and novel experience."

Farrington and Forster were perfectly willing to try the experiment which Watson hinted promised such interesting results, and it was agreed that each should take a dose of the powder before retiring, and meet together the next evening.

Promptly at the time appointed, the three men met in Watson's study, and after cigars had been lighted Watson asked Farrington to be the first to relate his experience, whereupon the Doctor drew from his pocket several pages of closely written manuscript, and began as follows:

An Aztec Mummy
Dr. Farrington's Story

I was standing in a museum looking at a case of mummies. One of them was marked "Mummy of an Aztec, found in a Cliff Dwelling," and it interested me very much. In size it was that of a small man, and was in a fine state of preservation, with the exception that the bones of the legs were exposed, and more or less disintegrated, in some places. The hands, even to the finger nails, were perfect, however, and there was a silver ring on the index finger. One hand grasped a large stone axe—the handle being modern. The right hand rested across the chest, clasping a necklace of silver wire.

"Interesting specimen, is it not?" said a voice at my side.

"Quite so," I replied. "But I doubt if it is really an Aztec mummy."

"What makes you think that?" asked the voice sharply.

"Because I don't believe the Aztecs buried their dead in Cliff Dwellings. However, it is an interesting mummy, and in a wonderful state of preservation."

I was so interested in examining the mummy that I had spoken without turning my head. Now, however, I looked up and saw a tall, gaunt figure of a man dressed in a suit of corduroy, and wearing a broad-brimmed hat, or sombrero, such as is generally worn on the Western plains.

"Well," he remarked, "in my opinion, it is a pretty good mummy. I made it myself, and ought to know."

"Excuse me, what did you say?" I asked, thinking I had not understood him aright.

"I said that was one of my mummies."

"What do you mean by that, sir?" I asked.

"You will understand when I tell you I was a dealer in curiosities, and during my time I furnished museums with a great many interesting and valuable specimens; when trade was slow, I occasionally helped nature a little, but that is all over now."

"Have you given up the business?" I asked.

"Had to; but perhaps you do not know that I am dead," answered my companion. "Fell from a cliff last year and broke my neck."

"Did you, indeed?" I answered, trying to appear interested.

"That's what I did. But let me tell you about that mummy. There was a scientific chap who came to our place and wanted to buy Aztec relics. Me and my partner made a trade with him and sold him a lot of stuff; but he was very anxious to be taken where he could dig some up for himself, 'to be sure of the authenticity and antiquity of the relics.' Well, me and my pard figured up that it might be to our advantage to take him to a good Cliff Dwelling, and we arranged that he should pay us so much for everything he dug up. If he found a mummy we got one hundred dollars; if stone hatchets and axes, two dollars each; arrow-heads, ten cents each; for stone *matats* and grinders, one dollar each, taking them as they came; and whole pottery, five dollars."

"Where did you find the mummy? Did you know of the cave?" I asked.

"Well, we knew where there were lots of caves, and where there were Indian graveyards. With the aid of a little stain and judicious arrangement of a body we prepared a fine Aztec mummy. Of course we used the body of an Indian, one who had been dead for a long time and was dried up and crumbly. My partner was a clever chap, and he fixed up the axe and the silver necklace, and we took the outfit and started for the Verde Canyon. We picked out a good-sized cave, and dug a hole in the floor, in which we carefully placed the mummy and covered him up with dry dust; then we wet the clay over him, leaving the floor hard and smooth as before. We also buried about fifty axes and two or three hundred arrow-heads, and half a dozen nice specimens of Indian pottery, which we burned up good and black.

"After we had 'salted' the cave to our satisfaction, we partly sealed up the entrance and returned to Flagstaff."

"Was that acting quite fair?"

"Fair? Why, how do you think that poor man would have felt if he had come all the way out to Arizona, and gone to all the expense of his car-fare and outfit, and then found nothing? It was philanthropy, my dear sir, the height of philanthropy."

"Was he pleased with the mummy?"

"Pleased? Why, bless your dear, innocent soul, he screamed with joy like a child, when we accidentally discovered a piece of a toe while digging in the bottom of the cave! He dropped on his knees and removed every particle of dirt with his hands, and almost cried over it. He carried on so that my partner nearly gave us away. He was a chump about some things: if anything pleased him, he would laugh, and his laugh sounded like the bray of a jackass.

"Well, sir, when this scientific chap got down on his knees, and commenced to paw the earth away from the fake mummy, my partner began to gurgle. I knew what was coming and punched him in the ribs, but it did no good. The scientific chap looked up and asked what was the matter.

"'Matter?' shouted my pard, and then he roared and yelled and howled.

"A look of doubt and annoyance came into our victim's eyes; but pard saved himself just in time.

"'Look!' he yelled between his paroxysms of laughter, 'look at that buzzard over there! I'm damned if he ain't the funniest buzzard I ever saw in my life,' and then he roared and yelled and jumped about. 'Look at him,' he laughed; 'see him fly! did you ever see anything so funny?'

"I am not sure but what the scientist thought he was crazy, but anyhow, he didn't catch on to what he was laughing at, and pretty soon went on with his digging. We stayed there three days and dug the whole place up and took back with us a basket full of stone axes, arrow-heads, three large prehistoric vases, and the mummy. He drove the wagon himself every step of the way, for fear something would get broken, and when we got to Flagstaff he spent two days packing the relics."

"Do you consider that sort of thing quite honourable?" I asked.

"Honourable? What is that you say, you squint-eyed dude? Now, my boy, don't get fresh with me just because I am dead and can't jump you."

I hastened to pacify him.

"Well, that's all right, but if you had said that to me last year when I was alive I would have marked squares all over your body with a piece of chalk and then played hop-scotch on you."

"I meant no offence," I said humbly.

"Maybe you didn't. But just you make another break like that, and I won't forget it; you will have to die sometime, and then,—oh, mamma!"

"Is your partner dead?" I asked.

"No, Jim is not dead by a long shot. I went down to see him last winter at his place in California, where he has opened up a new store. He has a good tourist trade—made a lot of money this year out of mermaids and sea-devils—there was a run on sea-devils this winter. He makes them out of fishes.

"The mermaids he makes out of fishes' tails and Indian children—robs the graveyards, you know. Some of them are really fine and artistic. I tell you he is an artist in his line.

"He has a branch store still somewhere in New Mexico, and made a stack of money last winter in Navajo blankets and scalp-trimmed Indian arms and shields. It is the scalp trimming which catches the tourist. He gets most of his scalps from California, from hospitals there; but when he is short, horse hair does pretty well, especially for old Indian scalps.

"And then, Navajo blankets. Holy smoke, a gold mine isn't in it! They make them of Germantown wool and aniline dyes, and they cost at the factory all the way from six bits to $10, and sell to the tourist for various prices; sometimes as high as $75 or $80. Oh, I tell you he is shrewd; some day he will be worth a million!

"Sometimes a chap goes into his shop and poses as an expert—those are the kind of jays that fill Jim's soul with joy. The fellow will pull over a pile of blankets, and after looking at them wisely, will say, 'Haven't you got any real good blankets? These are Germantown wool and mineral dyes.'

"Then Jim will say—'Ah, I see you know something about blankets.'

"'Oh, yes; a little,' answers the expert.

"'The fine old-style blankets are mighty hard to get now,' remarks Jim.

"'I know they are,' remarks the wise tourist, 'but still they are to be had sometimes, are they not? Come, now, haven't you got something choice hidden away?'

"Then Jim will look about, as though fearful that somebody might see him, and will steal softly into a back room and pull from beneath his bed a good cheap blanket—worth about $3—and spread it out lovingly in front of the tourist.

"'There,' he whispers; 'look at that; that is not for sale. I am keeping that for myself, but I thought you would like to see it, as it is very evident you know a good deal about blankets; isn't it a beauty?'

"Then the tourist 'bites,' and asks him what it is worth, and admires it, agrees with him as to the splendid old dyes and fine preservation of the native wool prepared in the manner of the old Navajo, speaks of its great rarity, and at last ends by asking Jim what he will take for it, and usually carries it away with him, having paid three or four times the value of a really good blanket.

"I've seen Jim pull their legs so hard they'd pretty near limp when they went out. Ah, those were happy days!"

The departed heaved a deep sigh, and gazed silently at his handiwork.

"Well," he said, "I must be going; I have a lot of things I want to do before morning, but hope to run across you sometime again. Glad you like the mummy. I forgot to mention that most of the teeth were gone when we first got it, and Jim put in a fine new set, and improved it a whole lot."

I glanced at the mummy, and when I looked up again, my companion had disappeared.

A Lesson in Chemistry
Mr. Forster's Story

I took the powder as agreed, and sat down to read the evening paper before retiring, with the result that I did not retire at all. I became much interested in an article on new explosives with which the Government has been lately experimenting, and had nearly finished it, when I heard a voice say to me, "Interesting subject, isn't it?"

I turned, and saw seated on my lounge a peculiar-looking man: his clothes seemed to be all run in together. You could make out the outlines of the man, but the figure was not clear; sort of foggy, you know. What surprised me most was that I could look right through him and see that back of the lounge.

I said to myself, "Is this a dream or the effect of the powder I have taken?" and I pinched my leg, and rubbed my eyes, but although I seemed to be perfectly wide awake, the shape did not disappear.

"What did you say?" I asked.

"I remarked that the subject of high explosives was decidedly interesting," answered the shape. "I was a chemist when alive, but it makes me sad to think how very little I really knew. Chemistry, as well as other branches of science, has made great strides during the past generation, since my day, but even now they really know very little."

"But," I answered, "it seems to me the high explosives which we now have are sufficiently powerful if we knew how to use them with safety."

"That's it," answered the shape. "Now, I have a couple of

hours to spare, and, if it would interest you, and you care to come over to my laboratory, I will be happy to give you one or two points which may prove of value to you—I say to my laboratory, but it really is not mine; I use any laboratory that is handiest, and I know most of the good ones in the city. You see, I do not need to have a key to enter a room; that is one of the great advantages we have, as you will discover one of these days. Just now I can get you in very well because the owner of the laboratory to which we will go is out of town. I will go in first and unlock the door for you."

I told him that I should be most happy to accept his invitation; it seemed the most natural thing in the world to be conversing with a ghost and to have him invite me to go to somebody's laboratory and use up his chemicals. It never occurred to me that it might not be considered quite good form. We went out of my rooms and downstairs, the shadow floating alongside of me in the most friendly manner possible. I could see by the position of his body that he had hold of my arm, but his fingers did not show on my coat-sleeve.

We went up town for perhaps half a mile, and entered a large brick building in which I noted were various studios. It was dark, but going up three flights of stairs my guide opened a door and ushered me into a large and extensively furnished laboratory, evidently belonging to some scientific man of means and experience. The ghost turned the button of the electric light, and then motioned me to a seat.

"My time," he said, "is somewhat limited, because I have an appointment with a lady at twelve, but I will show you what a high explosive really is, and then if we have time we will talk of something else. The difficulty about high explosives is not in making them, but in using them after they are made; you create a gigantic power which you do not know how to handle.

"The rather modern discovery of how to make liquid air has simplified matters a good deal. When you can make liquid hydrogen in quantities you will have a still better agent for many purposes. Now, let us take a little of this liquid air. You see it pours like water. As I happen to know, our absent host has nearly two gallons of it, or had this afternoon; some of it has evaporated, but, as you see, there is still more than a gallon left, and we will not steal much, as all we want for our experiment to illustrate to you the greatest explosive which can be manufactured is about as much liquid air as you can hold in a thimble."

"Do you propose to try your explosive here, Mr."—I hesitated. "By the way, what is your name?"

"Oh, call me any old name; it does not matter!"

"Mr. Spook, shall we say?"

"Ahem! a little personal, perhaps, but it will do as well as another. Now, as I was saying, I will show you how to make the most powerful explosive that was ever invented."

It is possible that I did not show as much interest and enthusiasm as he expected, and to tell the truth I was a little nervous. Spooks do not have the same interest in being careful in their experiments—an accident or two is of little consequence to them, but might be decidedly disagreeable to me. I may have shown something of what I was thinking in my manner, for Spook looked at me keenly.

"What is the matter? You do not appear interested."

"On the contrary," I answered, "I am deeply so, but do we not run considerable risk in trying such experiments in a laboratory without the consent of its owner?"

"Not at all, not at all. I will use a very small amount of the explosive, and there will be no damage done."

"Have you attempted to make it before, Mr. Spook?" I ventured.

"Oh, yes, last week; that was a mistake—you see now I know all about it, I didn't then; the explosion was something awful—it blew the building pretty much all to pieces. If I had been alive I don't believe you could have found a piece of me as large as your finger—they called it spontaneous combustion; however, we won't have anything of that kind to-night."

"Please don't," I answered.

"No, I promise you. Now we will take a little of this red

phosphorus—ordinary phosphorus will not answer—and pour a little liquid air on it, stirring it gently, as you see. Now, if I should let that dry it would explode at the slightest touch; but we do not want that, and we wish to increase its power, so we add a little chloride of potassium; now watch it dry—see the colour change to a light red-brown. There, if you should strike that or put fire to it, it would wreck this building as completely as if you had exploded fifty pounds of dynamite in it."

I drew away from the table instinctively.

"Have no fear, I will not explode it. Now watch me closely. I will ignite a minute quantity, about as much as would make the head of a small black pin or a No. 4 bird-shot. See, the rest we will put in this pail of water. There—now all is ready—here goes!"

He lit a match and touched the little brown dot—a tremendous explosion followed and the wooden table was split into pieces. The sound was so terrific and the shock so unexpected that I was dizzy and frightened.

"Great heavens!" I exclaimed, "you have broken everything in the laboratory!"

"No," replied the ghost rather shamefacedly, "not so bad as that, but I'm afraid that I have ruined the table and cracked a few things; however, I will be more careful next time: it is even more powerful than I thought. What do you suppose would be the effect on a warship if struck with a shell containing one hundred pounds of that stuff?"

I answered that she would be destroyed.

"Destroyed? I should say she would; the largest battleship would be blown to atoms."

The spook glanced at an old-fashioned Dutch clock in the corner of the laboratory.

"Fine clock that; glad I didn't break it with our little racket just now. I see I have nearly an hour to spare. Is there any experiment you would like to try?"

I said anything would interest me, but that I didn't care for any more explosives.

"I suppose you know how to make diamonds, don't you?"

I answered that for years men had tried to manufacture diamonds, but practically without success; that as far as I was aware they had only succeeded in making them so small as to be practically of no use commercially, and the expense of the manufacture was far in excess of their value.

"That's all right," answered the spook; "but really it is a very simple matter. Here; I will make a diamond for you." He walked across the room to the fireplace, and taking from the grate a lump of coal about the size of a billiard ball, he laid it upon the table.

"This," he said, "is nearly pure carbon, and as you are well aware it is practically what a diamond is. Now, I will illustrate to you how you may make a diamond from this piece of coal, which will be as good as any diamond ever found in the mines. We will manufacture it instead of letting nature do it.

"We will first place it in this glass bowl, and pour over it sufficient liquid air to cover it completely. We will let it remain until it is thoroughly cold, say, at least 200 degrees below zero; there—now all we have to do is to heat it and then subject it to a powerful—Great Gee Hosiphat! Five minutes to twelve! I must go—appointment with a lady at twelve. But I say, old fellow, just hold it under the blowpipe and get it hot—just as hot as you can; I will be back soon—ta-ta." His last words came to me faintly through the window—he had already floated out.

I took the queer-coloured piece of coal, and began heating it under the blowpipe. It did not burn, as I thought it would, but turned red and then white; gradually it seemed to grow larger and larger and brighter and brighter until I opened my eyes and found myself in bed with the sun shining full upon me through the open window.

An Interesting Ghost
Dr. Watson's Story

It is with the greatest difficulty, (said Dr. Watson), that I force myself to believe that what I am about to relate to you did not actually happen. It seemed to me that I was as wide-awake as I am at this present moment, and impossible that the strange series of incidents could be due entirely to mental disturbances. I went home and went to bed, after first taking the powder, and I think I went to sleep. How long I slept I do not know, but I was startled at finding myself floating about the room with much the same feeling as one has when floating in water, only it was without effort. My motion seemed to be governed entirely by my will,—if I glanced at anything in the room I would float towards it. Imagine my astonishment at seeing my body lying in the bed apparently sound asleep; you will admit the sensation was novel, to say the least.

After floating around the room two or three times enjoying the peculiar sensation, I began to wonder what they had been doing at the hospital during my absence. Immediately I found myself in the hospital ward. Dr. Ford and two nurses were standing by a cot at the north end, and glancing at the chart on the table I saw the patient was seriously ill.

"Moribund," said a voice.

"I'm afraid so," I answered. I turned and saw an elderly gentleman, dressed in the costume of the last century, floating beside me.

"Sad, is it not? People still die, I see, in spite of the wonderful advance in the science of medicine since my day."

"Were you a doctor when alive?" I asked.

"Well, I was called one, and received the regular license to kill or cure. I regret to say that I have since learned that I killed a great many more than I cured. The trouble is, after you are dead your patients know this as well as you do and say unkind things; even to-night I received word from a former patient of mine, and a ghost who ought to know better, to the effect that he intended to hunt me up and punch my head. I treated him for renal colic and he died of appendicitis."

"What sort of a death certificate did you give?" I asked.

"Heart disease, and let me tell you that was a great deal nearer to it than some of you chaps get nowadays."

"You are not complimentary," I said coldly.

"Perhaps not; but if you think my criticisms harsh and un-called for, let us get down to cold facts. Did it ever occur to you how very few people live to be even one hundred and twenty-five years old? You surely will admit that there is no reason why a man should not live to that age, barring accidents. We know that in Bible times there were lots of old fellows who passed their three hundredth birthday, and a chap named Methuselah claimed to be nine hundred and ninety-nine years old."

"Nine hundred and sixty-nine, was it not?" I asked.

"Perhaps you are right, but sixty-nine or ninety-nine, I am inclined to be a little sceptical about that record myself; there is one thing in its favour, however, and that is, that he made it an even nine hundred and ninety-nine, and not one thousand. Of course, you know there are plenty of people living to-day who are over one hundred years old, and some who have reached the very satisfactory age of one hundred and twenty-five; most of them, however, live in Bulgaria, Mexico, or some out-of-the-way place, and are so poor that they have to live abstemiously."

"Then you consider the secret of longevity to be a matter of diet?" said I.

"Partly that, and partly proper care of the nervous system; but come downstairs, and let us have a cigarette; I am dying for a smoke."

We floated down to the office, which happened to be un-

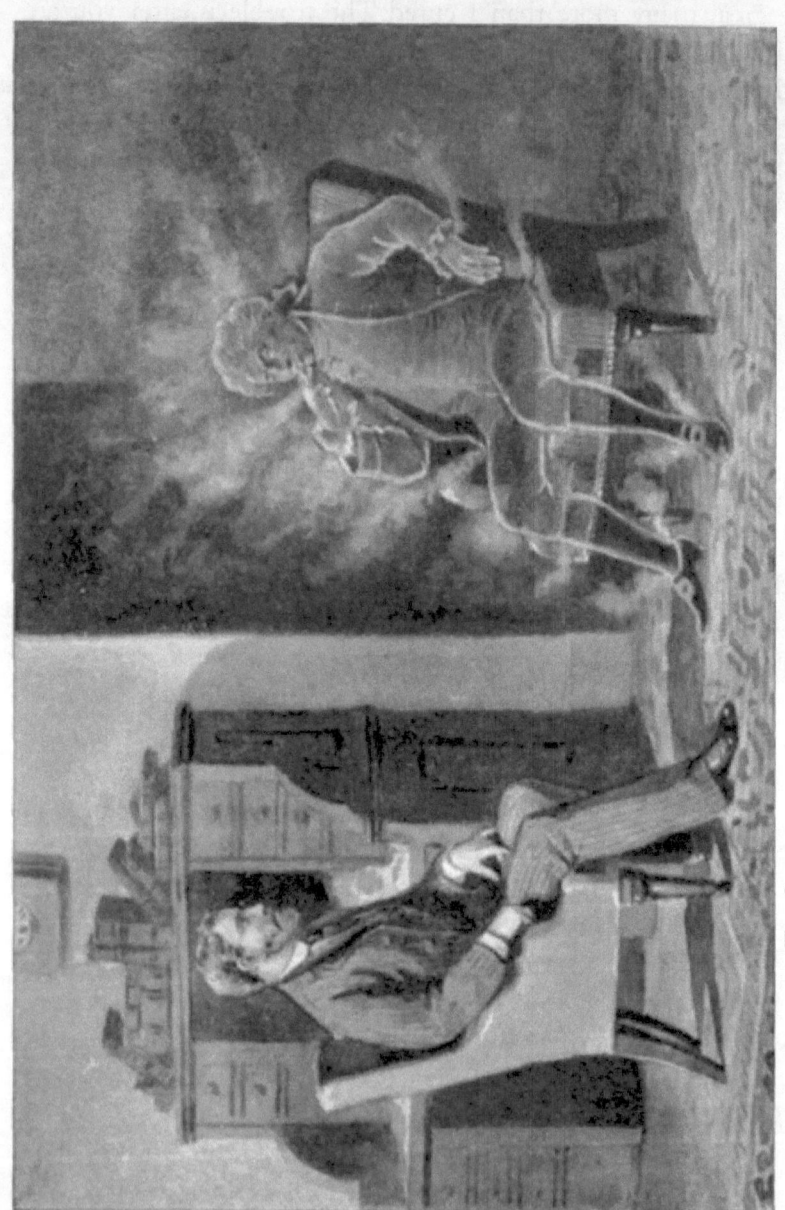

The Smoke continually oozed from All Parts of his Body

occupied at the time. The medical ghost helped himself to a cigarette from a trayful on the mantel-piece, and lighting it, he seated himself in an armchair, and puffed away with evident enjoyment. I noticed the smoke, which he inhaled continually, oozed from all parts of his body.

"My dear fellow," he said impressively, "you must understand that all diseases are caused by germs—microscopic bugs and plants, you know, many of them so small that they are invisible to an ordinary microscope, or, if seen at all, are not recognized. There are thousands and thousands of them, and each and every one has its mission in life, and preys upon and destroys other germs. Now, the human body is constantly getting a lot of germs inside of it which do not belong there. Some are taken in by the lungs, while floating in the air; some by the stomach, by the food and drink; some by the skin, etc.

"These germs are met by their natural enemies which live in man's blood—his body-guard, as it were—and are destroyed. But if the attacking army is very large, or from some reason the home army has been weakened and decimated, then the invaders flourish, establish themselves and wax powerful and strong, and the man becomes what is called 'sick.'

"Come," he said, rising abruptly, and throwing the unconsumed end of his cigarette into the fireplace. "Come with me to the laboratory, and I will show you in about two minutes more than I could explain if I talked for years, and a great deal more satisfactorily."

We floated down to the laboratory, and the ghost took from the shelf a wide-mouthed bottle and held it up to the light.

"Here," he said, "we have a culture. You, of course, understand how the germs of disease are cultivated for experimental use. It is needless for me to explain to you that certain media are used for these cultures, such as milk, beef-broth, etc.

"Here we have the germ of diphtheria, here of tuberculosis, here of typhoid fever, etc. That little short jar over yonder contains some cholera bacilli, which have been lately sent here. Now look at this typhoid germ. If we took a drop of healthy blood and put some of these typhoid germs in it, how they would wiggle! but if the drop of blood was from a typhoid patient, they won't wiggle very long, as you know. See this blunt-headed chap which we have to stain to see properly, even with this wonderful microscope; that is our old friend the bacillus of tuberculosis; but unless you see the patient first I do not believe you could distinguish him from the leprosy bug.

"These are known germs, but look through the glass at this drop, and you will see some bugs worth seeing, although the medical fraternity have not as yet discovered their value. Perhaps you know that most bacteriologists consider these germs to be plants, not bugs, although they admit some of them move a little. How astonished they would be if they could look through this glass! See that chap with green hind legs: he preys on the typhoid germ, and when they discover this physicians will simply inoculate the patient with a lot of these little chaps with the green legs, and they will do the rest.

"Here is a germ with yellow stripes which looks a little like a diminutive potato bug. He is the deadly enemy of the bug of consumption, and will attack and kill him on every possible occasion. They are about evenly matched, but I think the little striped chap is a bit the better. Another ghost and myself made a match the other night,—seven battles, the result to decide the championship,—a sort of a bugging main, as it were. I won. The first six matches were even. We won three each, but in the seventh my striped bug got the tubercular germ down and shook him as a terrier does a rat. The other ghost and myself nearly had a fight to get our eyes to the microscope. I tell you it was exciting. There is my champion bug now, see him?—the one with the fourth hind leg gone."

"But how," I asked, "are you going to prevent people from dying of old age?"

"Of course they will die of old age; but there is no such thing as old age under one hundred and fifty years; what you call old age is not old age at all. There are two kinds of old age or senility. Old age, properly speaking, results from a distinct modi-

54

fication of the nervous tissues and a hardening of the arteries—the former caused by unnatural conditions, nervous strain and dissipation, and the latter from over-feeding and drinking. The trouble with the ordinary man is that he absorbs great quantities of nitrogenous foods instead of making his diet one of nuts, fruit, milk, etc. In comparatively young men of the present age there is often a decided modification of the nervous tissues with symptoms resembling those in neurasthenia. In such cases galvanic treatment will restore the centres to their normal condition. You will, therefore, I think, admit that with proper diet and possibly the aid of a galvanic battery a man may live,—barring possible death by violence,—say, two hundred years."

"You mean," I said, "when we have learned to combat the various disease germs by pitting against them their natural enemies."

"Exactly, of course," answered the shade; "but it seems to me that we have talked long enough; I am becoming very dry, so let us repair to the Waldorf and have a cocktail."

"How is it possible," I asked, "that you can take a cocktail, there being nothing tangible about you?"

"Of course," answered the ghost, "it is impossible for me to actually drink a cocktail. I can, however, float over the bar and inhale the pleasing odours arising from the various concoctions served to the guests, and in my ethereal condition I enjoy the odours and am affected by them as much as if I were really drinking the liquid."

We floated from the house and down town, until we reached the brilliantly lighted Waldorf Hotel. There were many people in the bar-room, and the medical shade and myself, floating about over the different tables, inhaled with decided enjoyment the delicate aroma of the various mixed drinks so dear to the present generation.

To my annoyance my shade companion soon began to sing—he was evidently affected by the odours which had passed through him. His manner became familiar, and I had great difficulty in keeping him from kicking the glasses off the tables. At last I succeeded in getting him out of the room, and it was time, for as we floated into the street he began shouting in a most uproarious manner, and I was afraid that we should be arrested for disturbing the peace.

"Be quiet, I beg of you," I pleaded; "see that policeman on the opposite side of the street? We shall surely get into trouble if you make such a noise."

"Policeman?" hiccoughed the shade, "What the devil do I care for a policeman? Watch me go over and punch him in the stomach."

In spite of all I could do to prevent him he started straight for the officer, who was standing all unconscious on the corner, watching a pretty girl who was looking into one of the brilliantly lighted store windows. Now was my time to rid myself of this most undesirable companion, and I wished myself in my own room.

Instantly I found myself floating about over my bed, and there was my body sleeping as peacefully as ever. I was somewhat tired, but I remembered our contract to write down the result of our experiences, and immediately sat down to do it. After I had written it I read it over carefully to see if I had overlooked anything, and then wished myself in bed and asleep. The next thing I knew it was broad daylight. There, on my writing-table, were the pages of manuscript which I had written. They were real enough, whether the rest was a dream or not.

The Mound of Eternal Silence

"I ought to know something about it," said the Drummer, "for I went with the Prospector and the Eastern man to see Judson.

"I remember when we started out together the Eastern man asked the Prospector if he thought Judson was really crazy.

"'Yes,' said the Prospector, 'he is as crazy as a loon, as you will see when you get there.'

"'Tell me the story over again,' said the Eastern man.

"'Well, you see,' said the Prospector, 'they found him lying in the hot sand away off on the desert, with his head propped up against a rock, nearly dead for want of water. When they tried to rouse him he stared at them vacantly. They gave him a little water, and as soon as he had swallowed it he fought like a wild animal for more. It took three or four of them to hold him. He cursed and swore at them because they would not give him all he wanted, and his cries were pitiful. He alternately cursed and screamed for water, sometimes as loud as he could shout and then again in faint whispers.

"'Later on, when they dared to give him more at a time, he became tranquil, and towards night, after he had drunk a bowl full of thin oatmeal gruel, he went to sleep. When he awoke they questioned him.

"'He said that he had been prospecting with his partner, and had found a gulch with precipitous cliffs all around it where there was very rich placer digging. Directly in front was a high mound covered with big cacti, and they made their camp on the top of this. There was a little water in the canyon held in rock basins, and with this they washed out the gold and got a lot of

The Mound of Eternal Silence

it—Judson says three or four thousand dollars' worth. Then bad luck came, and the burro died. Three days afterwards Judson's partner was poisoned in some way, and died a few hours later, cursing Judson and saying he had poisoned him.

"'Judson buried him and also the gold; it was too heavy for him to pack, especially as he had no way to carry water. Then taking a small bag of gold dust in his pocket he started across the desert. He had a hobby for taking photographs and carried a small camera with him, and before leaving he photographed the place, which he called "The Mound of Eternal Silence," so that in case anything happened to him it could be found without trouble. They developed the negatives later, and he has them pasted all around his room. He called the place "The Mound of Eternal Silence" because during the two months he was there he never saw or heard a single living thing except jack-rabbits and a bird or two.'

"'What was that about his killing the dog?' asked the Eastern man.

"'Well, you see when Judson started off alone the dog would not leave his dead master, and sat upon the hill howling. Judson was afraid he would attract somebody's attention if they happened along that way, and after trying to get him to follow him without success, he went back and shot him. The first thing that Judson saw when he awoke the next morning after they had found him was the dog sitting on his haunches looking at him. Judson looked at the animal, but said nothing—something within him forced him to keep silence. After a time he snapped his fingers and called the dog by name.

"'Did you speak?" asked one of the men, Stevens it was, I believe.

"'I was only calling the dog," said Judson.

"'What dog?" asked Stevens.

"'Why, that dog, of course," said Judson, pointing at the animal.

"'You are crazy, man," answered Stevens. "The heat yesterday was too much for you; there is no dog there."

"'Judson turned away; he began to fear there might be something the matter with his brain, and that there was no dog there

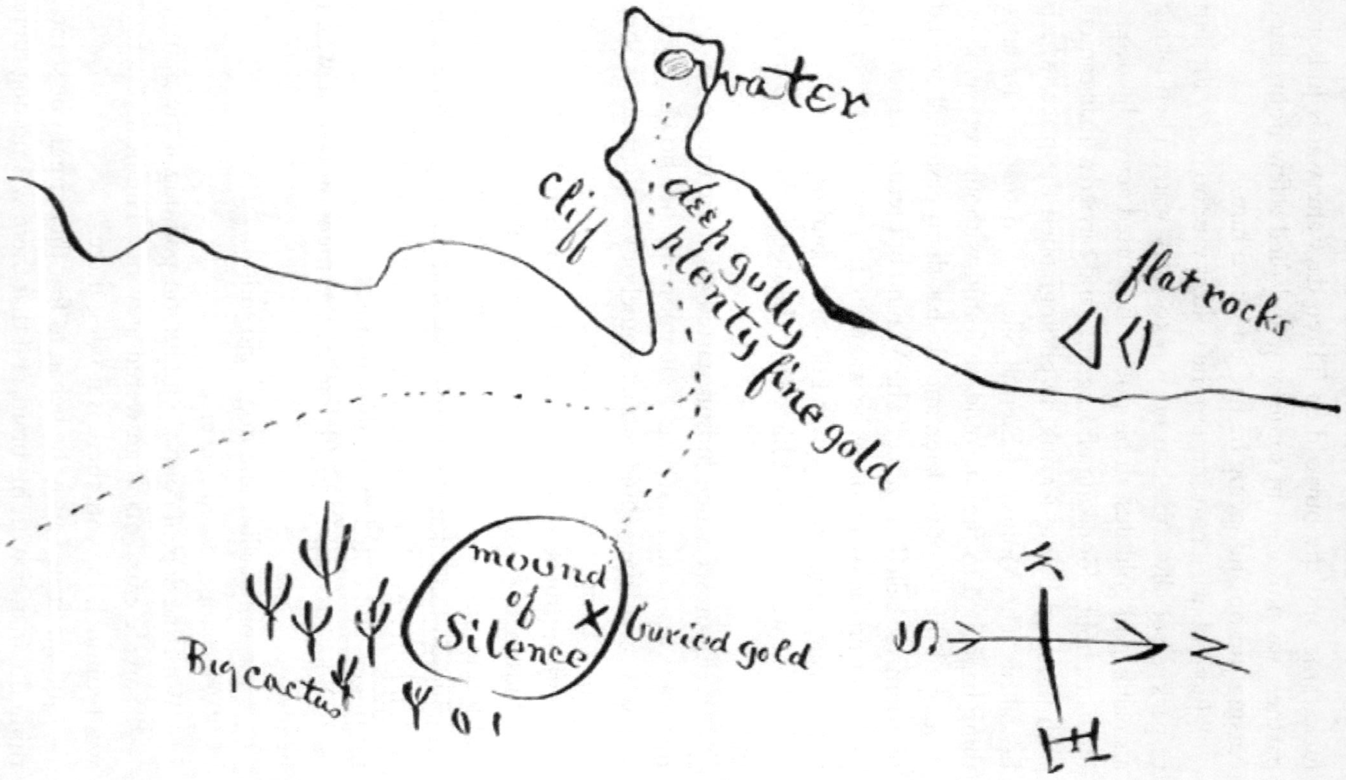

flat rocks △◊

crater

deep gully

plenty fine gold

cliff

N

W

S

E

mound of Silence

✕ buried gold

Big Cactus

after all. But when he looked again there he was as plain as ever. "I will take the brute outside of camp and kill him when I get a chance," he thought.

"'That evening when they made camp at a small water hole, Judson walked away out of sight and hearing of the camp. When he could no longer be seen he turned, and, aiming his pistol at the dog, pulled the trigger. The bullet hit the ground between the animal's legs, and he ran back a few paces and stood grinning at Judson showing his teeth, and his face looked like that of his old partner. Judson picked up a large rock and ran at the dog; the animal yelped slightly and started for camp. Judson increased his pace and the dog circled out into the desert.

"'Curse you,' cried Judson, 'I'll kill you yet.' Several times he threw stones at the animal, and twice he fell, bruising himself among the loose rocks. At last he sat down.

"'What is the matter with you,' shouted Stevens. 'What are you running about and shouting in that way for?'

"'That confounded dog of mine,' answered Judson unthinkingly.

"'Nonsense, man, there isn't any dog.'

"'Judson walked slowly back to camp followed closely by the dog. The men looked at him strangely. That night when he went to sleep the brute came and lay down beside him. A horrid fear took possession of him and he pushed the thing away, but it immediately crawled back again. At last he arose and spent the rest of the night walking up and down the desert, the dog following close at his heels.

"'When they arrived in Phoenix the doctor advised Judson to go to a quiet place and rest, and gave him an opiate.'

"'Why don't he go back and get the gold?' asked the Eastern man.

"'Because as I have told you whenever he starts to go back the dog meets him on the desert, and he is only free from it when he stays in Phoenix. He says the dog is his old partner, and will never let him go back there again. That is why he is willing to sell his secret.'

"'But how do you know if we pay him this money,' asked the Eastern man, 'that we can find the gold?'

"'Why, his map and directions together with the photographs ought to make it sure. Anyway, I am putting up $250 of my money with your $350, and run as much risk as you do; besides, you never would have known about it if it hadn't been for me.'

"'Won't he take less than $600?' asked the Eastern man.

"'Not a cent; I have tried him too often. If I had $600 of my own I never would ask any one to go in with me. It's a snap.'

"We found Judson seated in a big armchair, smoking a meerschaum pipe. His eyes had a peculiar wild expression, and he glared at us as we entered.

"'What do you people want?' he asked.

"'We have come to buy your claim,' said the Prospector.

"Judson laughed a strange, hard laugh.

"'Always the same—gold, gold, gold. Have you the money with you to pay for it?' he asked.

"The Prospector produced a bag of twenty-dollar gold pieces and shook it. 'Here it is,' he said, 'this gentleman and myself have made up the amount—$600.'

"'Well,' shouted Judson, 'give me the money and take the cursed claim, buried gold and all, and much good may it do you! I will go away—far away from here. My God, to think that I should sell a rich claim like that for nothing! But I wouldn't go back to it for all the gold in the world. Three times I have tried, and each time that dog devil met me at the edge of the desert, grinning at me with the face of my dead partner. Here are the photographs and the map, take them and go, my head aches; go away and leave me.'

"He buried his face in his hands, groaning and muttering to himself. The Prospector put the bag of gold on the table, and taking the photographs and map left the room. We followed him, closing the door softly behind us."

"Did you find the gold?" I asked.

"I didn't look for it," answered the Drummer. "They offered to let me in and give me a third interest for $300, but somehow

I didn't like the idea, and the whole thing seemed uncanny, and it is lucky I didn't. The Prospector and the Eastern man got back a week later without having discovered the 'Mound of Eternal Silence,' both mad as hatters, and each laying the blame of the failure on the other. I have always wondered since if Judson was really as crazy as they thought he was."

"Why," I asked, "what made you doubt it?"

"Oh," answered the Drummer, "I can't exactly say I disbelieve his story, but—well, you see, about a month afterwards I was in Phoenix again, and one night I saw the Prospector and the lunatic taking a drink at a bar together. A little later the Prospector passed me without seeing me. He was walking arm in arm with a stranger, and as they went by I heard him say, 'If I had the money I never would think of asking any one to go in with me. He calls it the "Mound of Eternal Silence...."'

"They passed on, and their voices were lost to me in the distance."

Story of a Bad Indian

Malita was a half-breed, the daughter of an old squaw man. She had spent several years at the Indian school in Phoenix, and had proved herself an apt pupil. Later she went to work on Simmons' Ranch. She was a very pretty, healthy looking girl, and one day Morgan Jones, the hunter and trapper, asked her to marry him. She went with him to his cabin near the Reservation and settled down.

Jones was a devil-may-care sort of chap, who, when he had a little money, came to the straggling one-horse town near the Reservation, drank considerable whiskey, and amused himself by running his pony up and down the one street, firing off his gun, and shouting at the top of his voice. This was Jones' idea of a good time, and his method of contributing his share to the sanguinary ornamentation of the embryo metropolis.

Malita made Jones a good wife, and attended to his creature comforts to the best of her ability, and when Jones returned to the cabin in an inebriated condition she soothed him, and put him to bed, looking upon such incidents as a matter of course. For a year or more they lived contentedly, and a little boy was born to them.

On the Reservation lived an Indian named Tixinopa, a splendid specimen of a savage athlete, and the most noted runner and hunter in his tribe. Like many of his race, while hating the white man, he loved the white man's fire-water, and it made him surly and quarrelsome. He was a natural leader, and often, at night, he spoke with fiery eloquence of the wrongs of his race, sowing the seeds of unrest and rebellion.

TIXINOPA

Tixinopa was the only cloud which disturbed the domestic horizon of the Jones family. He haunted the vicinity of the cabin, and was continually asking Malita for whiskey and tobacco when Jones was away, until at last Jones intimated to him gently that his presence was, to say the least, undesirable. Being a child of the woods and hills, he did not have at his command a large vocabulary of diplomatic phrases to enable him to do this politely, in fact, he was blunt.

In describing the interview to Malita afterwards he said:

"I told him if he cum around here any more I'd smash his head, an' he grunts an' draws himself up this a-way, and looks ugly and says, 'he's a big Injun,' and I told him to go to hell!"

For some time Tixinopa kept away from the cabin, but one day he appeared and demanded whiskey. He was half drunk, and his bloodshot eyes blinked at Malita as he swayed unsteadily in the doorway.

"No, Tixinopa, there is no whiskey."

Tixinopa's eyes grew ugly. "You lie, you half-breed squaw; but be it so, I will take the boy away until you remember where it is."

So saying he lifted the baby by the arm and swung him on to his shoulder. The child cried out with pain from its twisted arm. Malita's heart sunk with a dreadful fear.

"Give the child to me, Tixinopa, do not be so rough; see, you have hurt him."

She tried to take the boy, but Tixinopa pushed her away roughly and she fell to the ground. Up she sprang and threw herself upon him, trying to get the boy, and in the struggle she scratched his face slightly, so that the blood came. With a curse he struck her full in the face with his clinched fist and she fell as if dead, and lay with her hands twitching feebly.

"Take your half-breed brat," he hissed, throwing the baby roughly on the ground beside her. He turned to walk away, but something in the motionless form of the child caused him to look again, and he saw that his little head lay doubled under his arm in a way that could only mean one thing—a broken neck.

Malita rose unsteadily to her feet and looked about in a dazed

Malita

way until her gaze rested upon the little body of her dead baby; the next instant she was striking and cutting at Tixinopa, screaming like a mad thing.

The attack was so sudden and fierce that, trained athlete and fighter as he was, Tixinopa received a deep cut on the shoulder and a slight one on the arm before he succeeded in grasping her wrist, and twisting the knife from her. Then, seizing her by the hair, he drew her to him and drove the knife twice into her breast, throwing her to the ground, where she lay gasping her life away in broken sobs.

Tixinopa stood for a moment looking at Malita and was quite still. His arm pained him and he held up his hand and watched the blood dripping from his fingers. Then he took a self-cocking revolver from his belt and fired shot after shot into the bodies of the dead baby and the dying mother. Twice the hammer clicked on an empty shell before he ceased to pull the trigger, and he slowly turned away, pushing his empty pistol into his belt. As he did so he found himself face to face with Jones, but a different Jones than the one he had known. This Jones' face was white and drawn, and looked years older than the other Jones. The hand which held a pistol pointed at him shook unsteadily. A minute, perhaps two minutes, passed, and still the two men faced each other; then an evil light came into Tixinopa's eyes, and his hand slid slowly towards the handle of his knife, to be instantly smashed by a bullet from Jones' pistol. Another shot and the other arm was broken at the elbow. Neither man had spoken, but now Tixinopa began a low, wild chant. Raised to his full height, with his broken arms hanging by his sides, he chanted the death song of his people, the same song which had been sung by his father, and his father's father, and for generations past by all the dying warriors of his tribe.

"Tixinopa," the voice was a husky whisper, "for her sake I won't torture yer as I would like ter,—God give me strength to keep from doin' it!—but I'm afeared He won't unless I kill yer quick. All I hope is that if there is a hell, your black soul will roast in it for ever and ever, amen!"

The muzzle of the pistol was now within a few inches of the naked breast; still the low, wild chant went on, the bronze figure standing as if turned to stone. Then another shot and the chant stopped.

* * * * * * * *

Ten minutes later a horseman rode slowly into the desert. To his left, as he crossed the half-dry bed of the alkali stream, two Indian boys were skinning a rabbit alive and laughing at its agony. From afar back on the other side of the valley he heard the strains of the "Star Spangled Banner" played by the pride of the Reservation—the Indian band!

A Queer Coincidence

"You say," said Doctor Watson, as he rested one arm on the mantel and looked thoughtfully at the open fire,—"you say there is no proof of the actuality of what is called telepathy or thought-transference, and perhaps you are right, but I have several times in my life had experiences which were very difficult to explain except by some such theory, and if you care to listen I will tell you one of them which I have in mind."

Our chorus of approval evidently left no doubt as to our desire to hear the story, for Watson smiled, and lighting a fresh cigar he began as follows:

"On the seventeenth of January last year there was a slight wash-out on the Northern road not far from Chicago, and the forward trucks of one of the cars on train 61, on which I was a passenger, left the rails, but luckily the train was going slowly at the time and there was little damage done except a general shaking up of the passengers in the car as the forward wheels bumped roughly over the sleepers for a few yards before the train stopped. The other cars did not leave the track, and only one man was seriously injured.

"This man had been standing on the platform at the time and was thrown between the cars and badly crushed. I was close to the end window and saw him fall, and when the conductor called for a doctor I responded at once.

"I found the man lying on a blanket surrounded by a number of the passengers. He seemed to suffer but little pain, and I feared, from a casual examination, he was badly injured internally, although he was perfectly conscious; he was bleeding at the mouth, and his legs seemed to be paralyzed. He asked faintly if I thought he was going to die, and I cheered him up, as is customary in such cases, but shortly afterwards he developed such serious symptoms that I felt forced to tell him I feared he was seriously hurt, and it was quite possible he would live but a few hours.

"Upon hearing this he became very much agitated, and whispered to me that he wished to speak to me alone, saying he had something of the utmost importance to communicate.

"I thought it was probably some message to send to some members of his family, or some instructions regarding his affairs, but after a few words I became very much interested. He talked for fifteen minutes, part of the time being sustained by the use of stimulants. His story, which was a very strange one, I will repeat as nearly as possible in his own words. After repeatedly asking me to assure him there was no possible chance of his recovery he said:

"'It is not necessary for you to know my name, but it is sufficient for me to tell you that I received a good education in my youth and graduated with high honours at one of the large universities in this country. I always had more or less interest in the study of physiology, and during my college course conducted a series of experiments in hypnotism, and made some interesting discoveries regarding the exaltation of the senses, and especially in relation to illusion and hallucination by the aid of post-hypnotic suggestion.

"'It had been my earnest desire to occupy the position of professor of physiology in one of the universities, but failing to obtain a position of this kind, and having no means of support, I gradually became poorer and poorer, earning a livelihood as best I could, until I became discouraged and attempted to make money in a way not quite so honest.

"'The idea suggested itself to me during a series of experiments which I had conducted with a friend of mine. It so happened that this friend was paying teller in one of our well-known banks of Chicago, where he is to-day. He is a thoroughly honourable man in every way, but I found that he was a good hypnotic subject, or sensitive, as we call it. At first he could not be considered first class, but he was much interested in the subject, and allowed me to hypnotize him repeatedly. After a few evenings he became very easily influenced and one of the best subjects I had ever had. I could put him to sleep in a moment, simply snapping my fingers and telling him I wished him to sleep; of course this can only be done with sensitives who have been repeatedly hypnotized.

"'Under these conditions I succeeded in making him do very many wonderful things, especially in the way of post-hypnotic suggestions; a post-hypnotic suggestion is a command given to hypnotized subjects that at some future time they perform a certain act. In most cases, in waking from the hypnotic sleep they have forgotten that the suggestion has been given them, but at the time set they perform the act unconsciously, as though by their own volition. Not only will they do this, but after the act is performed they usually sink into a quiet sleep,[1] from which they awake after passing into the normal sleep, and, as a rule, have forgotten that they did anything unusual, or that they have been hypnotized, and take up the thread of thought again at the point where they first entered the hypnotic condition. They do not remember what they have done or seen. Their mind is a blank as to all that occurred during the time they were hypnotized.

"'For the last two years I have been rather fortunate, in a small way, speculating in stocks. My capital being small, the amount of money I could make was, of course, comparatively little; yet I succeeded in doing very well until about three weeks ago, when, by two or three unfortunate speculations, I found myself absolutely destitute, and without a penny in the world. It was then the idea suggested itself to me to hypnotize Mr. Herrick and make him bring me money from the bank. This of course was perfectly possible, if no accident occurred, or no unforeseen difficulty presented itself, which I had not previously thought of,

---

1: This is unusual; the subject rarely falls asleep after carrying out a post-hypnotic suggestion unless commanded to do so.

as the cashier would act simply as an instrument, being governed entirely by my directions. I asked him in a casual way several times about the affairs of the bank, and learned one day that the bank would have an unusually large balance in settling with the clearing-house. It was the custom for Mr. Herrick to lock up his own funds, and simply state to the cashier that he had done so.

"'According to a carefully arranged plan, I hypnotized him last evening and commanded him to take all the money and securities he had in his possession, after settling with the clearing-house, and instead of locking them in his vault to put them in a bag, of course taking precautions to do this when no one was observing him, and then leave the bank in the usual manner.

"'He was to take a carriage and drive directly to a small, unoccupied house which is situated on the corner of Blank and 117th streets.

"'It was my intention, as I had gone so far, to go still further. I knew that Mr. Herrick would bring me the money and securities, and that I should find him asleep in the house, but what I did not know positively, and what I feared was, *that he might not forget what he had done when he awoke.* As a rule, sensitives obey the command to forget, but in the course of my various experiments I have found sensitives who had a vague idea of what occurred, perhaps nothing tangible, but still sufficient, in a case like this, when there would be a great row about the lost securities, to suggest a possible clue.

"'It was a very cold day, six degrees below, I think, and I had deliberately intended to leave Mr. Herrick asleep after I had taken the money from him and let him take his chances, sleeping without any fire or covering, in an hypnotic condition, with the temperature below zero, and you can judge what his chances would have been. This scheme I thought out deliberately, and what seems strange, I had not the least repugnance against arranging for the death of my friend. After I had once made up my mind to make him steal the securities his disappearance seemed to be the only way to insure my safety. Of course no one could know I was connected with this matter.

I would not go near the bank, and unless he was followed, which was most unlikely, as he had been with the bank some years and was a thoroughly trusted official, there would be absolutely no chance of my detection.'"

Watson relighted his cigar, which had gone out, and continued—

"While he had been speaking another train had arrived with a lot of workmen who were busily engaged jacking the car back on the rails. The train was about to return to Chicago, so I inquired the name of the bank and its president, and the address of the house, writing them down so there could be no possible mistake. I then hastened on board the train, leaving my patient under the care of Dr. Morse, a local physician, who agreed to notify me as to the condition of the man later in the day.

"Upon arriving in Chicago I immediately drove to the bank, but found it closed. I was told, however, that Mr. Bartlet, the president, was attending a corporation meeting in an office in the same building. I immediately hunted him up, and, upon hearing my story he hastily ordered a carriage and we drove to the house as described.

"On our way out we stopped and picked up Dr. Marsh, who as you know is very much interested in such matters. It was quite a long drive, but we found the place without difficulty. It was unoccupied, and many of the windows were broken, and altogether it presented a very dilapidated appearance, such as the cheap houses on the outskirts of a great city often do after having been unoccupied for a year or two. We tried the door and found it unlocked. On the first floor the rooms were entirely empty, loose papers scattered about, and no signs of any one having entered the house. Upon going upstairs we found the door on the first landing at the head of the stairs closed, but not locked. At the back of the room was a cracked wooden stool and a dilapidated hair sofa, which had evidently been considered too used up to be of any value. Part of the cover was torn away, one of the legs was broken, and some of the hair stuffing was lying scattered about the floor. On this lounge lay

Mr. Herrick apparently sound asleep; his lips blue with cold, his face pale, and the general appearance of a man half frozen to death. He was breathing very quietly, however, and his heart action was still fairly good, although somewhat slow. By his side lay a small bag, which, it is needless to say, was pounced upon by Mr. Bartlet. It contained some valuable securities, and a great bundle of bank bills of large denomination. Both Marsh and I considered Herrick's condition as decidedly interesting and unusual, and we were both of the opinion that, as part of the story had proved true, it was very likely the whole would turn out just as described.

"If this proved to be the case, all that now remained to be done was to restore Herrick to his normal condition, which might or might not be easy to accomplish. The first thing to be done was to get him out of such a low temperature. We tried various methods of restoring consciousness, but without success. What we did not like was that his heart action was gradually becoming weaker. We gave a hypodermic injection of *strychnia*, and the heart was soon acting in a much more satisfactory manner. There was no return to consciousness, however, so taking him in the carriage we drove back to Dr. Marsh's house, and arriving there we all turned to and did what we could to restore Herrick to consciousness. Now that he was in a warm room the drawn expression and the blue look left his face, but otherwise he appeared to sleep as soundly as ever. The heart was now acting very well, and aside from the coma the condition of the patient gave us no cause for anxiety. As time went on, however, and we absolutely failed to waken him, and the heart again showed signs of weakness, we began to feel somewhat uneasy.

"You see," said Watson, "we did not know what suggestion was given the patient; these post-hypnotic suggestions are peculiar in their action upon some sensitives. If, as it is fair to suppose, this man was ordered to sleep, he should in the natural course of events sleep for a number of hours and then awake, after passing from the hypnotic sleep to the normal sleep; but we know very little of the effect on some nervous systems of post-hypnotic suggestions. Another thing, in many cases the patient will not waken or cannot be wakened except by the person who put him to sleep. The reason for this is plain enough. Part of the effect on the mind of hypnotic suggestion is due entirely to sleep. The skilled hypnotist commands one of his sensitives to sleep under certain conditions. The sensitive expects to be awakened by the same voice and in the same way, and habit and association have fixed in his mind certain conditions which he associates with the order to awake. There is no doubt whatever that Mr. Herrick heard what we were saying when we spoke to him in a loud voice, but he heard it without understanding, much as a person in a sleepy condition hears noises about him without trying to comprehend them. It is undoubtedly true that the man who put Herrick to sleep could have wakened him in a moment, while we, with all our knowledge and experience, were unable to make his brain regain its normal condition. We decided to let him sleep; and if, at the end of a few hours, he did not regain consciousness, we would try again what we could do to assist him, of course watching the heart in the meanwhile and using nitro-glycerine or *strychnia* if indicated.

"At that moment Herrick suddenly spoke, at first huskily and then in a loud, clear voice, shouting, 'Yes, yes, I hear you; I am awake.' Then he sat up, asking in a dazed way, 'Where am I? What does this mean?'"

"As he did so the old-fashioned clock in the hall struck the hour of seven."

The queerest part of this story is suggested by a letter received from Dr. Morse the next day, which read as follows:

Dear Watson: You asked me to write you about the injured man, and I do so now to tell you he is dead. He died a minute or two before seven o'clock last evening; I know the hour exactly, because I was watching him at the time, and for some moments he had been whispering and muttering to himself, but all I could catch was something

about, "I withdraw my command;" when, suddenly raising himself, he shouted, "Wake up, wake up!" and fell back
dead just as the clock in the church-yard struck seven.

I should be much interested to hear whether his story was
true or not. Drop me a line about it when you have time.

Very sincerely yours,

F. Morse

Story of an Insane Sailor

"That pocket-piece of yours," said the doctor, "reminds me that I have an interesting one of my own; perhaps you can tell me what it is." He took from his pocket a silver coin and handed it to Jennings, as he spoke. One edge had been flattened, and a hole pierced in it.

"Ah! an old Spanish piece," said Jennings, "evidently of the time of Pope Leo Fourth, sometime in the sixteenth century. A very interesting piece. Where did you get it?"

"There is a curious story connected with that coin," meditatively remarked Dr. Watson; "perhaps you would like to hear it."

We had been dining with Watson and were now comfortably seated in the library before an old-fashioned open fire. It was snowing outside, making the warm, bright study all the more cheerful by contrast.

"Perhaps you remember," said Watson, "that during the winter of 1886 I devoted much more of my time than usual to the Insane Asylum. I was very much interested in testing the value of hypnotism for insane patients, especially mild cases and those having illusions and insistent ideas. I had been quite successful in one case—a woman who had tried to starve herself to death under the impression that the devil commanded her not to eat was greatly benefited by post-hypnotic suggestion. Suggesting that the devil would not come any more induced pronounced hysteria, but when hypnotized, and told that the devil commanded her to eat, instead of to abstain from food, she took nourishment readily, and soon developed an extraordinary appetite.

"An immediate improvement in her condition was notice-

ONE EDGE HAD BEEN FLATTENED AND A HOLE PIERCED IN IT

able, and as her general bodily health improved, the illusions became less and less frequent, and she was discharged from the asylum as cured in less than three months."

Watson paused and gazed meditatively at the end of his cigar. "Ever tried to hypnotize an insane person, Jennings?"

"Not that I remember."

"You, Morris?"

"Can't say that I have."

"Hm! Well, sometimes you succeed, and sometimes you don't; more often you don't. There was one patient, a man by the name of Allen, who had been a sailor. He was subject to fits of extreme melancholia, and at times was positively dangerous, as he imagined some one was trying to poison him.

"I never succeeded in hypnotizing him, although I tried repeatedly. However, I saw him every day, and as his general health improved, his attacks of melancholia became less frequent. He seemed grateful to me for taking an interest in him, and often talked with me about his early life and the out-of-the-way countries he had visited. Shortly after I was called away and did not return to the asylum for two weeks, and when I did go back I found that Allen was dead. He had cut his throat one afternoon with a large pocket-knife and made a mighty clean job of it, too.

"Well," continued the doctor, "among his effects they found a package addressed to me, which contained a letter and a silver coin. The coin you now hold in your hand, the letter I have here in my desk."

He opened a drawer and took out a large yellow envelope containing a number of pages of closely written manuscript.

"This letter," said Watson, as he slowly turned over the pages, "contains a story so strange that I did not for a moment believe it had any foundation in fact; but during the past year or two I have learned certain things which have caused me to change my opinion. Whether the story is true or not we will, of course, never know, but I *now* believe that it is a true record of events which actually happened. I have made some inquiries and find that the places mentioned do exist, or did at the time this story was written, and—but never mind; I will read you the letter and you can form your own conclusions:

"Dr. S. T. Watson:

"*Dear Sir:* I have made up my mind to kill myself, but before I die I wish to make a confession of my wrong doings, as *he* insists that I shall and I dare not disobey him. I therefore write this confession, to be read by you after I am dead.

"You tell me I *imagine* I hear the voice and see the man. I tell you, doctor, you who think me crazy are the one who is deceived. You do not believe in telepathy and thought-transference, and yet I could tell many times when you looked at me of what you were thinking. I tell you that I hear Jim's voice as plainly as I ever heard yours, and he talks to me and tells me that he will never leave me while I live, and then he laughs. Oh, that laugh! He comes often at night and wakes me out of a sound sleep with that awful laugh, and then he whispers to me to go to sleep again. Of course you do not believe in spirits or ghosts, and you believe I am crazy, and that the half-invisible form of my dead partner which comes to me and talks to me, and whose voice I hear as plainly as I ever heard yours, exists wholly in my imagination. Well, doctor, you have been kind to me, and I hope and pray you will never suffer the way I have suffered during the past three years.

"Just three years ago to-day I was on board the *Ada Gray*, a small schooner off the coast of Florida, bound for the Isthmus. There were seven of us in all, including the captain and mate, the latter an old pal of mine who had arranged to get me in as one of the crew. In some way he had learned that the captain was to take with him some two thousand in gold, and although we had no plans, we intended to get the gold in some way. On our way down we had talked over many schemes, but none of them seemed satisfactory. The gold was kept in a small fireproof safe in the captain's cabin, but it was an old-fashioned key-lock affair, and we did not anticipate much trouble from that quarter, even if we could not find the key. The great point was, how we were to get the money and get away. At last we decided to drug the men's coffee, and when they were sleeping from its effects, we would take the money and leave in the schooner's yawl, in which, as the weather was very calm and the Florida coast could be seen in the distance, we should have no difficulty in making the shore.

"Jim had overhauled the medicine chest and had found a vial containing a lot of morphine pills marked one-eighth grain, and as neither he nor I knew how much morphine it took to drug a man, he watched his opportunity and emptied the contents of the vial into the coffee.

"After supper we kept on deck for some time waiting results. At last Jim went forward and reported everything quiet and the men apparently all asleep. We found the captain in his cabin lying on his bunk breathing heavily. The key to the safe was in the captain's pocket, and we opened it without difficulty. There were six rolls of twenty-dollar pieces marked two hundred dollars each, eight rolls of ten-dollar pieces, and a bag of silver.

"We took the money and some other things we found in the cabin, including a pair of revolvers, a double-barrelled shotgun, and a rifle, and put them in the boat, together with a small keg of water, tinned meat, and a bag of ship biscuit. After these were carefully stowed away in the yawl, Jim went back to the cabin, while I busied myself arranging things in the boat. He soon came on deck again bringing several bottles of brandy, and coming to the side of the schooner reached them one by one to me over the side. As he handed me the last bottle I saw the burly form of our negro cook rise slowly out of the hatchway, rubbing his eyes as if half asleep. Jim saw my stare of surprise, and, turning quickly, faced the negro, who was looking at us with a dazed expression. He could not have drunk of the coffee, for I have since learned the amount of morphine Jim put in the pot was more than enough to kill the entire crew.

"Jim turned, and, walking slowly up to the man, said hoarsely: "Go down," at the same time pointing to the hatchway.

""What for?" asked the negro, moving a step backward.

""None of your business what for; go down, I tell you."

""I don't take no orders from you, nohow," answered the man. "Where's the captain?"

"'Without a word Jim struck him full in the face with all his strength. The blow was an awful one, and the negro staggered back, and would have fallen had not he brought up against the foremast. He roared with rage, and came at Jim with a rush like a mad bull. Jim bent sideways, and something flashed in his hand, as he struck upwards under the man's arm.

"Instantly the negro stumbled forward, and fell on the deck, and then sat up and began to cough. He coughed incessantly, like a man who has swallowed something which choked him. Jim looked at him a moment, and then, without a word, cast off the painter and jumped into the boat. There was not a breath of wind, so we each took an oar and pulled towards the faint line of land just visible in the western horizon.

"The schooner lay almost motionless, with the silence of death about her. The negro had stopped coughing, and all was still, save the faint creaking of the masts and spars and the sounds of our oars in the rowlocks.

"In the west the sun-painted clouds lay in great masses of gold and purple, tinting the sea with ever-changing colours.

""Damn pretty sunset!" remarked Jim, as he drew in his oar, and bent over to light his pipe, and then, musingly: "I wish I hadn't had to kill that nigger."

"Shortly after dark a gentle breeze sprung up from the south-east, and we put up a little sail we had brought with us.

"Fowley Rocks light was in plain sight, and about midnight we rounded Cape Florida, and entered Biscayne Bay, and by daylight we made the mouth of the Miami River, where we tied up to a small pier, owned by a man named Brickle. On the other side of the river stood a long, low stone building, which, they told us, was once used as a government building, and was called Fort Dallas.

"We told the people we had come from Key West, following the coast along inside the keys, and were on a hunting and fishing trip. Upon inquiry we learned that there was very little game about the bay except crocodiles, but that we could get splendid sport by going up the river into the everglades and following the shore line north to New River. They advised us to get an Indian to go with us. This plan suited us exactly, as once having disappeared in the wilderness we could come out at some other point, and having assumed new names could go forth into the world in perfect safety.

"Before starting we bought a light flat-bottomed boat for use in shallow water, and after rowing up the river a few miles we made camp and burned the yawl, first breaking her up with our axes. This took up the greater part of the day. In the afternoon Jim went up to the head of the river and reported meeting an Indian who told him of a large island which was, as near as he could judge, about thirty miles to the north, on which there were deer and turkeys.

"We had plenty of provisions, and for three days we pushed our boat northward among the islands of the great grassy lake. In many places the water was so shallow we had to push our way through grass and reeds. We noticed a great many white flowers growing on the banks of the islands, and water-lilies were abundant, but they had no smell.

"Towards evening, on the third day, we landed on a large island on which there was a high mound. Hundreds of white herons and various other kinds of birds were nesting in the trees, and there were a good many ducks about. We shot some of the herons and cut off the long hair-like plumes, but the flesh was strong and unpalatable. The ducks, however, were very good.

"We camped on the mound, which was much higher than the rest of the island, and decided to stay there for a day or two. While putting up the tent I saw something shine, and picked up a silver coin which had evidently been worn as a medal, as one edge had been flattened and a hole pierced in it. There was no date, but it was evidently very old.

"That day we tried fishing, and shot several ducks. We had but one shot-gun, so took turns with it at the ducks.

"That evening Jim produced an old pack of cards from his pocket and suggested a game of poker. My luck went against me from the beginning, and when we stopped playing I had lost fully two-thirds of my share. The next morning I awoke feeling remorseful and sulky, and demanded that Jim play another game to give me a chance to get even. He assented readily enough, but my bad luck continued, and in an hour I had lost all of my money and had nothing left to bet. Jim got up, taking the gun, and went down to the boat to repair a leak which had bothered us the day before. I sat on a log, inwardly raging and cursing myself for my foolishness. The rifle was leaning against the log near me, and involuntarily I took it and dropped the lever to see if it was loaded. It was empty, and the hammer moved back and forth at the touch of my finger. Evidently the spring was broken. But how? Why? I felt in my pocket for my revolver with feverish haste. Gone. Then I understood!

"I rose and walked slowly down the slope of the mound, and nearly stepped on a large rattlesnake which lay coiled up beside a palmetto root. I looked at the snake as he lay there watching me, rattling angrily all the while, and then I looked at Jim's coat which hung on a branch near by, and at the doctored rifle in my hand, and the more I looked the more wicked thoughts came into my mind. I glanced towards Jim; he was apparently busy with the boat, and I could just see the top of his back as he bent over. I hastily fastened one of the dead herons to a stick and held it in front of the snake, which immediately struck it in the breast, and then uncoiled and slowly retreated into the scrub. Taking two pins from my coat, I inserted them into the holes made by the fangs of the rattlesnake, and took them out covered with blood and poison. In a few minutes this dried, and I then fastened the pins inside the arm of Jim's coat in such a way that his hand would be scratched when he put it on.

"This done, I hung the coat back on the branch and walked off a little way, but feeling more than half inclined to go back and take the pins out again while there was yet time. Perhaps Jim did not mean to kill me, but simply wished to protect himself against treachery on my part;—but then I remembered the negro and the morphine, and—well, dead men tell no tales. As I turned to go back, I saw Jim in the act of taking down his coat, and I felt a queer choky sensation in my throat and a sort of half catch to my breath as he pushed his arm through the sleeve, at the same time putting the back of his hand to his lips in a way that could only have one meaning. I watched him with an ugly feeling of satisfaction, wondering how long it would take for the poison to begin to take effect.

"Jim put a couple of sticks on the fire, and then sat down on a log and commenced to fill his pipe, but soon laid it down. "Curse it!" he said; "I feel queer."

"He got up and walked up and down, rubbing his arm. He looked at me in an odd sort of way once or twice, and then went into the tent and lay down. Shortly after he called to me, and on my going to the door of the tent he tried to rise, but fell back and became delirious, laughing and shouting my name, and muttering to himself. He breathed with difficulty, and in a little while became unconscious, and just as the sun was sinking over the faint line of trees in the west he died.

"I took down the tent and dug a hole and buried him where he lay. I built a huge fire and sat by it all night without closing my eyes. Towards morning the moon came up and the sounds of the night noises ceased, and as soon as it was light I put the gold and what things I needed in the boat and made haste to leave the island. I paddled for two or three hours before I noticed that the sun, which had been to my right when I started, was at my left, and I knew that I must have turned the boat around.

"I turned about and paddled on steadily all day long, but night found me with no signs of dry land anywhere, nothing but an unending stretch of grass and water as far as the eye could reach.

"When it grew dark I lay down in the bottom of the boat and tried to sleep; but as soon as I closed my eyes I felt cold all over, a creepy sort of cold, and heard voices whispering. At first I told myself they were not voices, 'twas a trick of my imagination, the wind, perhaps, or the rustle of the grass about me; but then I heard Jim's voice. There could be no mistaking his horrid, sneering laugh; it made me afraid, but do what I would I could not help hearing it. I stopped my ears and wrapped my head in my coat; but still, from time to time, I could hear the voices whispering, and Jim's laugh, and at times I felt cold.

"The next day I poled and paddled until late in the afternoon. I felt very hot, and my head ached as though it would split. I had a pain in the back of my neck and drank a great deal of water. I knew I had some sort of a fever, but having no medicine I could do nothing but push on, hoping to find my way to dry land.

"All that day I continually heard Jim's voice laughing at me, and the next I knew I found myself in an Indian camp, and was told that I had been found in the boat sick. The gold was gone; the Indians claimed it was not in the boat. One of them seemed to be a chief and wore a big turban on his head with a silver band around it. They told me his name was Tom Tiger.

"And now, doctor, good-by. Jim is whispering to me again and telling me it is time. In five minutes after I sign this I shall be dead. I shall make no mistake. My knife is very sharp.

"*John Allen*"

The Elixir of Life

"Behold," said Doctor Watson, "the Elixir of Life!"

Robinson looked up from his writing and assumed an expression of deep interest.

"Wonderful! I have often heard of it. Is it the true *Elixir vitae* of the ancients, or a new and more subtle compound?"

"Listen, scoffer; if you will behave with a decorum consistent with the gravity of the subject, I will explain how I became the possessor of this wonderful powder. Perhaps in your life of seclusion and deep toil you may not have noticed this advertisement which has appeared for the last month regularly in the morning paper?" Watson took from his pocket-book a newspaper clipping and read as follows:

METHUSELAH CLUB

The object of this club is to enable its members to live to be one hundred and fifty years old. All persons desiring to become members should apply for particulars to Rengee Sing, No. — Twenty-seventh street, City.

"Are you a member?" inquired Robinson.

"Not as yet, but Jones is, and it was through Jones that I came into possession of this mysterious drug. It seems that Jones decided after reading the advertisement that he would like to become a member of the club. Jones' health is not very good, as you know, and he called on Rengee Sing, and the result of the interview was that he came away with this small vial of the wonderful Elixir, for which he paid twenty good dollars. He was so impressed by the gentleman who sold him the powder that he came to me, as his medical adviser, to ask my opinion as to the advisability of taking some of it. He brought with him a paper purporting to be the translation of an ancient papyrus manuscript, the original of which was in Tibetan or Sanskrit and which was ingenious, if fraudulent. He told me a rambling story of how this Rengee Sing had procured this powder, and the whole thing was so peculiar that I decided to interview the gentleman myself; but first I made a point of getting our friend Strauss to analyze the powder. His report of the analysis shows it to be composed entirely of chloride of sodium or common salt, with a small quantity of some unknown vegetable matter which gives it a yellow colour. Armed with this information, I called upon Rengee Sing at his office on Twenty-seventh street."

"You interest me," said Robinson, glancing at his work, and palpably attempting to suppress a yawn.

Watson arose, and gently but firmly removed the pen from Robinson's fingers; he then placed a book on the papers, and continued:

"The office was distinctly oriental, and there were numerous Bokhara and other good rugs scattered about; besides there were gorgeous divans, and the air was heavy with peculiar Eastern odours. I was admitted by a gigantic negro dressed in oriental costume, and another negro arose as I entered, and stood respectfully at the inner door. I asked for Rengee Sing, and was informed that he would 'be at liberty in a few moments,' and 'would I sit down and wait,' all in very good English from one of the gigantic sable guardians who bowed me in. I was kept waiting but a few moments, when the door opened and a small black-bearded Hindu came softly into the room dressed in the ordinary European costume. There was nothing striking about him except his eyes, which were really the most wonderful eyes I have ever seen in a human being. With the gentle manner peculiar to his race he smiled and asked me to take a seat near the window."

"Is it possible?" said Robinson, languidly, lighting a cigarette.

"Is what possible?" inquired Watson, frowning slightly.

"Why, that he asked you to take a seat near the window."

"Robinson," remarked Watson sternly, "remember that your mental infirmities will not prevent my punching your head if you interrupt me with any more foolish questions."

Robinson grinned, and after ostentatiously placing a paper-weight within easy reach, Watson continued.

"I inquired if he was the person to whom I should apply for information about the Methuselah Club.

"He answered that he had the honour of being the president of the club, and would be glad to supply me with all information in his power. Did I wish to join?

"'A friend of mine,' I said, 'has already become a member, and the description of a wonderful powder has interested me, likewise the history of the powder.'

"The Hindu smiled gently, showing his white teeth, and said that he was not surprised at my curiosity. He then went to a desk and took from it the printed circular which Jones had already shown me, and which was supposed to be a translation of the ancient manuscript. It is the one I hold in my hand; please glance over it before I continue my story."

Robinson took the paper.

"What is this hieroglyphic affair at the top here?" he asked.

"That," said Dr. Watson, "is probably a copy of some very ancient amulet or talisman. The fish at the bottom was often used to designate '*Dag*,' or the master; next above we have the Solomon's seal, then the four Chaldaic letters *Jod-He-Van-He-Iaho*, which is 'The Deity;' the other symbols are strange to me."

"Ah," said Robinson, "a weird sort of thing, is it not?"

"Don't be sarcastic, read it," sententiously remarked Watson.

Robinson did so.

"'Let him who dares to live forever take of the powder, but let him think of "*Aum*;" but speak it not on pain of death; let absolute "*muckta*" be known to him; let him study the secret "*mantras*," and ponder on the mysteries of "*Vach*;" let him also say each day in his prayer "*Aum ma-ni pad-me hum*."

"'He who takes of the powder three times should acquaint

himself with *khet dalet* the *marcaba* and the *lah gash*, then he will
never die. Even though he wished to live a thousand years, so
it shall be!'"[2]

"Well," remarked Watson, "what do you think of it?"

"Fake," answered Robinson.

"Verily, out of the mouths of babes, etc.," said Watson, "but,
O learned friend, you have not heard the whole story. Listen. I
asked Rengee Sing if he would be good enough to explain to
me fully about the powder and especially how and where he
obtained it.

"'My dear sir,' he said, 'I see you are a scientific man, and it
always gives me great pleasure to meet such, and to explain to
them as fully as possible how I, Rengee Sing, obtained possession of one of the most valuable treasures in the world, the Elixir
of Life; but before doing so I must enrol your name among the
members of our Society; in fact, one of the rules of the Society
is that unless a person becomes a member we can tell him nothing, beyond allowing him to read the circular which you have

2: Translation of the sacred manuscript found with the "Elixir of Life."

already seen. The initiation fee is five dollars, and you are at liberty not to take the powder if you desire not to do so after you have become a member, but if you wish to become a member in high standing, and to take the powder, which will insure you a length of life far beyond that of ordinary mortals, an additional fee of twenty dollars is charged for the powder.'

"I decided," continued Watson, "that the experience was worth five dollars, so I intimated that I should be delighted to become a member of the Society, and handed Mr. Sing five dollars, whereupon he wrote me a receipt and gave me a member's card, which stated that I was a member of the Methuselah Club of the second class, and entitled to receive the Elixir, and to become a member of the first class upon the further payment of twenty dollars any time within the next ten days. After which, if I had not been made a member of the first class, my name should be dropped from the rolls.

"Rengee Sing was the embodiment of courtesy when he bowed low and handed me my receipt.

"'My dear sir,' he said, 'I shall now be happy to explain to you anything that I can.'

"'I would like,' I said, 'if possible, to see the original papyrus which I understand was found with the Elixir, and I also would like to learn more fully the details as to how and where this Elixir was obtained.'

"Rengee Sing bowed, and, going to the corner of the room, opened a small fireproof safe, taking from it a roll of what proved after being unrolled to be an ancient papyrus manuscript written in the Sanskrit language. As far as I could make out it seemed to be the original of which the printed circular was a translation. It certainly appeared ancient enough.

"'This manuscript,' said Sing, 'and the box of powder was obtained by my brother and given to me at his death. He died from the effects of a fall from his horse, which broke three ribs and otherwise injured him internally. He never would have died except from the accident, as he had taken several doses of the Elixir. Just how long it will enable a man to live we do not know, but certainly one hundred and fifty years and perhaps even two hundred years. He obtained it in the following manner: My brother had long been desirous of visiting Lassa, which is, as you know, the wonderful capital of Tibet, but was unable to do so until a few years before his death, when he accompanied a Hindu who went there for the purpose of making certain reports to a foreign government. His name I am not at liberty to disclose, but his report was simply signed Punjaub A.B. My dear brother described Lassa to me very minutely, and from all accounts it must be the most wonderful city in the world. As you probably know, no European or Christian has ever been allowed to enter within its walls. According to my brother's description the city is situated in a fertile plain on the Sampo river some six hundred miles north of Calcutta, and has a population of fully sixty thousand persons. The streets are wide, and the houses have their walls whitened and the frames of the doors and windows coloured red and yellow.

"'Nearly west of the city, connected with it by a splendid avenue, is the mountain of Buddha, where now stands the temple of the Grand Lama. This temple is four stories high, and therein dwells the Grand Lama and his High Priests. Some idea of the magnificence of this temple may be obtained when I tell you that its great pillars are covered with plates of pure gold. The Grand Lama can live forever, and many people believe he does so, but he really does not. After a certain time he reincarnates himself into a new body. All of the priests, however, are very old. It is claimed the *Pandita* is at least one hundred and fifty years old. The Grand Lama has about him two priests of the highest grades, one the *Pandita* and the other Tchoiji. The Grand Lama sits upon an altar or throne for hours at a time, clothed in gold-woven cloth and jewels of fabulous value. Over his head is a magnificent peacock's tail composed entirely of gold and precious stones. It is the custom of the Grand Lama to receive persons who desire to receive his blessing at certain hours of the day. For a small amount of money one is allowed to bow before him; for a little more one may touch his garment, and receive his silent blessing; but for the sum of twenty *rupees* he will speak to the person and touch him with a little wand. The Punjaub A.B. in describing his interview states that the Grand Lama talks in a hoarse voice which he tries to make as much as possible like God's.

"'It was during his visit to the temple that my brother learned of the wonderful treasures preserved there, fabulous stories being told about a huge emerald with an ancient inscription engraved upon it,—the mystic seal of the first Lama, which had been handed down for ages, together with the greatest treasure of them all, known as the Elixir of Life.

"'The wonderful powder was and is used by the high priests, some of whom are of great age. It is supposed to have been brought into Tibet by King Srongb Tsan, during the seventh century, and that it originally came from Nepal.'

"'How did your brother procure it?' I asked.

"'By bribing one of the priests. My brother was wealthy, and being very desirous of procuring some of this wonderful powder, he tried to buy some of it. Under no circumstances, however, would they listen to him or even allow him to see it. He succeeded, however, as I said, in bribing one of the priests, paying him a large sum of money, several hundred *rupees*, I believe, and was shown the sacred chests containing this powder, and other treasures, including precious manuscripts and some jewels of great value. The powder was contained in five little gold boxes, of beautiful workmanship. While examining them they heard a door close and the sounds of footsteps in the passageway. The priest became very much frightened and begged my brother to replace the boxes and manuscript at once, and was so agitated that he did not notice my brother when he slipped one of the gold boxes into his pocket. The person, whoever he was, passed on down the passageway, and as soon as they dared they hurriedly left the vault. Luckily for my brother he left Lassa with the Punjaub that evening, and never learned whether the theft was discovered or not. Probably his powder would have done him little good had it been so and had he been suspected.'

"'But how,' I asked, 'do you know that this Elixir will really prolong life?'

"Sing smiled sweetly, and said, 'I myself, my dear sir, am a living proof of that; I am one hundred and ten years old, and to-day there are in New York some sixty men who will live to that age, having taken the powder, unless they die from some form of disease. This elixir will not protect them against poison or diseases where the poison germ has entered the system. That is impossible; but it acts upon the nerve centres and upon the blood corpuscles in such a wonderful way that there is no degeneration. The person simply lives along the same as he would between the ages of thirty and forty; he is always the same. He may die from many causes, but it would not be from old age.'

"'My friend,' I said, 'took the liberty to analyze some of this powder.'

"'Ah! And may I inquire the result of his analysis?'

"A peculiar yellow light came into those eyes, and although he smiled—Have you ever seen a caged tiger languidly looking at the crowd of people in front of his cage suddenly discover a dog near him?"

"I don't know that I have," said Robinson.

"Well, if you do you will notice the same yellow light flash into his eyes, and the sudden change of expression that I saw in the eyes of our friend Sing. It was gone in a moment, however, and he was again smiling sweetly.

"'I understand he found it to consist principally of common salt.'

"'Quite so,' answered Sing; 'but he must have discovered that it also contained something else?'

"'That is true,' I answered, 'there was a small amount of vegetable matter which gave it a yellow colour.'

"'That is the true Elixir,' said Sing; 'salt is merely necessary for the results. You, as a scientific man, know that the poison which kills so quickly from the fang of a cobra and the ordinary white of an egg can hardly be distinguished by the chemist. He finds them both to be albumen.'

"'Why, then, should one kill and the other be harmless?' I asked.

"'Simply the minute "something else" which is contained in the snake poison and which is held in solution by the albumen.'

"'Have you any other proof of the power of this Elixir?' I inquired.

"'My dear sir, I trust you do not question the truth of my statement regarding my own age.'

"He frowned slightly, and those wonderful eyes of his glanced like lightning towards the two huge attendants standing in plain sight in the hallway.

"'Not at all,' I hastened to assure him. 'It all seems so wonderful to me, you must excuse my apparent incredulity.'

"'The most natural thing in the world,' smiled Sing with grave courtesy, 'but I will let your own eyes banish any doubt you may have as to the wonderful properties of this strange powder.

"'Ashmed,' he called, 'ask my son to come here a moment if he will be so good.'

"The attendant who had spoken to me when I entered immediately disappeared, and in a moment a back door opened and the bent figure of a very old man entered the room and spoke to Sing in a weak voice. The language was evidently Hindustani, but I caught a word here and there which sounded familiar. Sing spoke to him sharply, and turning to me said, 'This is my son; he is nearly eighty years old, but refuses to take the powder on account of his religious principles—he belongs to the sect who believes that to die is better than to live, that his spirit will become incarnate in another body, and in his next life he will be at least a Kobtchie.'

"My eyes must have betrayed my incredulity.

"'You do not doubt that he is my son?' sweetly asked Mr. Sing.

"'Certainly not,' I answered.

"'I trust, then, that I shall have the pleasure of furnishing you with some of the wonderful powder? There is not very much of it left, but luckily it requires a very small dose. I have enough probably to supply one hundred men to insure them existence for one hundred and fifty years. When that is gone the supply can never be replenished.'

"He sighed.

"'Thank you,' I answered. 'I shall think the matter over and in all probability give myself the pleasure of calling upon you again.'

"Then I came away, being bowed out by the sable attendants with all ceremony possible. There! What do you think of that?"

"Do you intend to return and purchase the powder?" asked Robinson.

"Perhaps," answered Watson, "but I think I will wait awhile and see if Jones lives to be one hundred and fifty!"

The Voodoo Idol

Jones lay on the sofa watching the consul mix a long, cool drink of Apollinaris water and crushed sour-sop. His arm pained him a good deal and the bandages felt hot and uncomfortable. By his side was a little table on which were piled numerous articles in a manner common to mankind, among which were a bottle of whiskey, a revolver, several books, and a plate containing some bananas and sapodillias. A light breeze stirred the curtains behind him, and under the awning he could see the long stretch of green palms and waving cocoanuts, back of the city. A faint white line indicated the road to Lecoup.

"I tell you what, old man," said the consul, as he poured the mixture from the shaker into the tall, thin glasses, "you are almighty lucky to get out alive, and you took big chances. Stealing a god of the Voodoo priests is about as dangerous an experiment as playing with fire over a barrel of gunpowder. From your description I should judge the place you found it was about fifteen miles back of Gantier."

Jones nodded in silence.

"Well," continued the consul, "it was somewhere in that vicinity they killed that Frenchman last year, and how they ever let you get out alive I don't know. They meant to kill you fast enough, tried to poison you at Gantier, and knocked out that servant of yours. You escaped by not drinking the coffee. Then some one shot at you on the road, and even then you did not have sense enough to throw away the idol; but even if you had I don't know that it would have made any difference. Then the day before yesterday they put a bullet through your arm at Lecoup, and if old Chabeau had not gone himself with you part of the way, I do not believe you would ever have reached here alive. What on earth made you monkey with that idol anyway?"

Jones explained that he could not resist the temptation to steal it. He had been camping on the banks of a nearly dry stream, ten miles or more east of Gantier, where he had found the little hummingbird, *Mellisuga minima*, the smallest bird in the world, very abundant. He had also trapped a specimen of the extremely rare *Solenodon*, and being anxious to procure more he had stayed there for several days. Within half a mile of his camp was a small stone tower open at the sides, in the middle of which stood a little idol on a sort of pedestal. This little idol was about eighteen inches high and was carved out of stone, the eyes oddly enough being bone. Jones had cast longing glances on this idol, but did not dare to touch it, or in fact to go into the tower, as the natives were sullen and suspicious, and on more than one occasion showed signs of being decidedly ugly.

Jones saw enough to confirm his impression that these people were a bad lot, and one dark night he "folded his tent like the Arabs and silently stole away," taking with him as a souvenir the little idol, which he had carefully rolled in a blanket and packed on one side of his pack-horse to balance his box of specimens on the other. Fear of possible unpleasant consequences had caused Jones to ride fast, but he had been followed and three separate attempts made on his life by unknown persons. The last one resulted in a bullet through the upper part of the left arm. He was safe enough now, however, as he remarked, there being little likelihood of danger while under the protection of the American consul in the city of Porto Prince.

"Don't you be too sure of that," said the consul. "There, try that and see how you like it."

Jones sipped the cool mixture; it seemed like nectar to him in his feverish condition. The bullet which had passed through his arm had made a wound, which, while not in itself serious, had left him weak and feverish.

"Yes," continued the consul, "you were mighty lucky to get off as you did. You may not know it, but right here in Haiti the people in the interior are as savage and bloodthirsty as any Central African tribe. Most of the inhabitants are descendants of negroes brought from the Gold Coast many years ago. They have reverted to their original wild state, keeping up many of the ancient customs. Mixing as they have with the Indians of the interior, the present race is even worse than their ancestors. From Toussant l'Overture in 1804, when he first ruled, to Hyppolite Florvil and Salomon, the island has been the scene of continuous insurrection, intrigue, and murder.

"Salomon was probably the best of them all. He was an immense negro, some six feet four inches tall, with a pock-marked face, who had received an education in Paris and married a Frenchwoman. He, like the rest, however, was superstitious and cruel at heart. Hyppolite was a Voodoo priest and, it is said, an anthropophagist. The people of the interior have an intense hatred for the white man, and still retain many of the barbarous customs of the savages of the African interior.

"The Voodoo dance is presided over by a high priest, who usually commands a goat or a hen to be killed, but in some of the more important ceremonies a child is murdered, and its blood mixed with the *tafia* and drunk by the dancers. The high priest is called *Papoloy*. Every two years after the dance of the moon a human sacrifice is ordered; generally a young girl is killed and eaten. You probably ran up against one of the Voodoo gods, and the large stone in front was undoubtedly the sacrificial stone. How you ever got away alive passes my comprehension. They evidently thought that you would try to leave in the daytime, and had things all arranged for taking a shot at you somewhere, but your nocturnal skedaddle knocked their plans galley west. There is one thing dead sure, those Voodoo priests are bad medicine, as we used to say out West, and you want to keep your weather-eye open until you are safe on board a steamer and out of the harbour. I wouldn't give five cents for your life if you walked about the streets of Porto Prince. When the time comes to leave I will have you smuggled on board. The authorities would wink at your assassination, but they would not openly countenance it."

Jones remarked wearily that he had begun to believe it might be as well for him to rest quietly in the consulate, and not give them another chance.

The soft flower-scented breeze blew softly in through the open window and was soothing to Jones. Lying there on the lounge with his eyes closed, he soon fell asleep, and the consul left him to attend to his various duties. When Jones awoke he lay in a sort of drowsy condition—half asleep and half awake. Through his partly open eyes he looked through the open door leading out on the broad piazza. There was a chair in front of the door, and over the top of this he saw a face and a pair of very black eyes looking at him intently. For a moment he imagined it was some freak of his imagination, as the face was as still as though it was carved in wax. Right in line with Jones' eyes, and within a foot of his half extended arm, was the little table, and the handle of the revolver seemed to stand out as though placed there for his especial benefit. That was certainly real, and it required a very slight movement for his fingers to close over the pistol handle; but he did not move and lay watching the figure, which began to rise slowly and developed into the form of a large, ugly-looking negro. Jones remembered particularly noticing a white scar across the cheek just under the eye. The man was not looking at him now, but was glancing about with the stealthy look of a hunted animal. At the same time he drew from under his coat a long, unpleasant-looking knife. As he did so Jones lifted his pistol, and, aiming hurriedly at the breast, fired. The man dropped, grasping at the chair as he did so, but immediately rose to his feet, swaying unsteadily. Bang! went Jones' pistol again. This time the negro did not fall, but stood seeming half dazed, steadying himself by holding on to the back of the chair. Jones fired again, and at the report the man clapped his left hand tightly over his heart, and with a muttered imprecation threw the knife at Jones just as he fired his fourth shot, the thud of the knife driving deep into the wood close to Jones' head being followed by the sound of a falling body on the hard floor. As the consul ran into the room followed by one of his men he found Jones sitting on the lounge, pale and weak from excitement and fever.

"Lucky you had the pistol," remarked the consul; "might have been unpleasant. See that gummy green stuff on the knife? Well, that is poison, and a mighty bad poison, too; one little scratch—But all's well that ends well; the steamer is in, and if I were you I would make a bee line for the pier, and get on board just as soon as the Lord will let you!"

Jones rose with some difficulty and went out upon the wide balcony. On the blue waters of the bay he saw a large steamer, and at her stern, floating in the breeze, the most beautiful flag in the world, the Stars and Stripes.

The effect on him, in his half hysterical condition, was to make him want to cry and cheer at the same time. The room he had just left was dark in contrast to the bright sunshine outside; but he could see the knife and the dead body of the negro, from which a narrow dark red streak was slowly making its way across the floor.

"We can't go any too quick to suit me," said Jones.

An Arizona Episode

1

Wendell Harrison was a club man with no ambition in life beyond making his small income pay his club fees, and leave enough for him to live in the manner peculiar to young men of his class. His one hope in life, as he often told his particular crony, was to find a rich wife, and it seemed to Harrison that chance had played into his hands when he received an invitation from old John Stiversant to join his party on a trip to the Grand Canyon in Northern Arizona.

Harrison had met old Stiversant on the yacht of a mutual friend a few weeks before, and knowing how to make himself agreeable he had done so to the best of his ability, with the result that he had been asked to make one of a party on this western trip in Mr. Stiversant's private car.

"Good luck to you, old man," said his chum as he was leaving the club on his way to the station. "Go in and win."

"Trust me for that," answered Harrison.

The trip out proved a delightful one. Miss Nellie Stiversant, the young lady who, Harrison had decided, was the most likely catch, did not prove as easy as he imagined. While charming and agreeable, she had evidently seen more or less of the world, and was not to be gathered in by the first man who made up his mind he would like to have her ornament his home. Likewise, she was a girl with common sense, and knowing her position and advantages did not lose her head when a man showed an inclination for her society. In fact, just before the party arrived in

Flagstaff she had made it very evident that she did not care for serious attentions from any one. She was, however, of a decidedly romantic nature, and Harrison pondered deep and long as to the best method of gaining her affections. Late that evening he was reading a sensational novel, when suddenly he laid it down and a far-away look came into his eyes.

"By Jove," he muttered, "the very thing—on this very road too. Whether the story is true or not, it is reasonable enough, although a trifle dramatic, but that is what is wanted to attract a girl like Nell. She don't care for me and never will, and all she wants is excitement and novelty, but if she thinks I saved her life or risked my own in protecting her, there might be a chance. In this story the chap had led rather a tough life, but had reformed, and the road-agents recognized him and knew he meant business. He got pretty well shot up, but the whole thing cast a halo around him, which would undoubtedly attract any romantic girl. Damn it, why couldn't I do it? It is that or nothing, the trip will be over in two weeks, and it is pretty evident that I am not in it unless something extraordinary happens."

2

The saloon was pretty well filled with a sprinkling of miners, Mexicans, and ranchers. Men in blue overalls, flannel shirts, and wide-brimmed hats were playing the different games of chance or standing in groups in front of the bar. A harsh brass-sounding piano on a raised platform at the end of the room was being played by a short-haired individual in a dress suit, and a young lady who evidently did not object to the calsomining process to aid nature was singing a topical song. In the corner stood Wendell Harrison surrounded by four rough-looking men, who seemed very much interested in what he was saying.

"Now I think you understand thoroughly what is required," said Harrison. "I am to pay you five dollars each now, and twenty dollars each when the job is done, likewise if it comes off successfully and the bluff works I am to give you twenty dollars more upon our return to Flagstaff. Don't forget to carry out the plan exactly as we have agreed. When I spring from the coach waving my pistol and firing blank cartridges, one of you is to shout, 'Fighting Harrison, by God!' and shoot two or three times as you run. The thing is easy, but requires a little judgment. I do not care where you stop the stage. Stop it any old place, but not too near Flagstaff. I shall be alone in the coach with an old man and two young girls, so there is not the slightest danger, and I will see that the old man is unarmed.'

3

"Say, Jimmie, I must tell yer something, but let me larf first. Say, I nearly fell down in a fit. I am going to tell yer all about it, but don't call me a liar, or I'll kill yer. What do yer think? Oh, Lord, how my stomach aches!—what *do* yer think? Wait a minute—I'll tell yer in a minute, let me larf it out now, or I shall drop down right here!

"Say, I sat in that booth over there having a quiet drink, and what do yer think? A dude in the next booth commenced putting up a job with four ducks; one of them is Mexican John and the other is Brady, our assistant bar-keeper here. As far as I can make it out Brady got the three other ducks. Say, wait a minute! I don't believe I ever will stop larfin'. What do yer think? this dude is going up to the Canyon on my next trip, and is going to have these four fellers stop the stage to put up a bluff on his girl to show what a fighter he is, and he is to give um twenty dollars each. He is going to jump out and pull his gun and clean out the crowd, and then go back and bask in the sunshine and admiration of the young girls. Oh, Lord! The skunk don't care how much he scares the girls and the old man who are goin' along, but all he wants is to pose as a fighter from away back. But say, Jimmie, what do yer think? I have been thinkin' this thing over, and I don't believe his little picnic will transpire. He calculates to blow in eighty dollars to make a monkey of himself, and I am thinkin' that we can use that eighty dollars in our business and teach the fellow a good lesson all ter wonce. What breaks me up more than anythin' is that he told Brady to hunt me up and tell me on the quiet that there was a reformed desperado going with me who used to be known by the name of 'Fightin' Harrison.' Worked me into the job too, see? What do yer think?"

4

The stage was slowly toiling up a dusty hill some five miles from Flagstaff. The road was rough and the day was warm. The stage-driver let the horses take things easy, and from time to time shook with suppressed emotion. "I hope I may die," said he to himself, "if this ain't the damndest."

In the back seats the two young girls, the old man, and the would-be hero were enjoying the scenery and the novelty of the trip in spite of the dust. Suddenly three men sprang into the road, and a loud voice commanded the stage to "hold up."

"What is the matter?" asked Nellie excitedly.

"Don't be afraid," said Wendell, pressing her hand, "remember I am with you."

A rough-looking man appeared at the side of the stage.

"Is your name Harrison?" he said, addressing Wendell.

"It is," answered Harrison boldly; "what do you want?"

"I have a bill here for eighty dollars against you, which will have to be paid or you will have to get out and go back to town with me."

"What do you mean?" gasped Harrison.

"Just what I say, young man; your name is Wendell Harrison, isn't it? You used to be known here by the name of 'Fighting Harrison,' didn't you?"

"Certainly not, you have the wrong party," answered Harrison indignantly.

"Well, I don't know about that; didn't somebody tell you that this fellow was 'Fighting Harrison,' Bill?"

"They certainly did," answered the stage-driver.

"It is all a mistake," said Harrison.

"Mistake or not, you will have to pay or go back to town with us; that is all there is to it. I believe you are the Harrison I want."

"Oh, Mr. Harrison," said Nell, "do pay this man and let us go on; you can easily recover the money when you go back to town."

"Yes," said Mr. Stiversant, "that certainly is the best way to settle the matter; it is, undoubtedly, a case of mistaken identity, but this man is evidently acting in good faith, and you will have no difficulty in straightening matters upon your return at Flagstaff."

Harrison's face was very red, and he looked and acted ugly; but this man evidently meant business, and there was no way out of it but to pay the money, which he did with a very bad grace, taking a receipt made out to Wendell Harrison, alias "Fighting Harrison of Arizona."

"An exciting incident," said Nell, as the party rode away.

"Yes," said Harrison, "but one that might just as well have been left out of the programme."

The stage moved on, but Harrison seemed uneasy; every few minutes he mopped his face with his handkerchief and pressed his hand to his head as if in pain. Visions of the little reception committee some few miles ahead were constantly in his mind. What would he say and do when the stage was stopped, and he received his cue to spring out and fire off his six-shooter, especially as he had only fifteen dollars left in his pocket. What would these pseudo-gentlemen of the road do to him, if, after his little exhibit of bravery, he failed to wind up the melodrama by settling with the actors? He didn't care to find out, and his mind was bent now in deciding the best way to get back to Flagstaff. He continued mopping his face, and once or twice he groaned.

"What is the matter?" asked Mr. Stiversant; "are you ill?"

"I fear so," answered Harrison faintly. "I have a dull pain in my head and I feel faint."

"Oh, let us go back," said Nell, "it is only five miles, and we can start again to-morrow just as well."

"Perhaps it would be as well," said Harrison weakly; "I fear I am going to be ill."

In the privacy of a room at the hotel Harrison hastily manufactured an urgent telegram calling him at once to San Francisco to see a sick uncle, and had barely time to explain matters and express his deep regret at being forced to leave the party at such short notice.

An hour later he lay back in a luxurious chair in the smoking compartment of the California Limited, and gazed out of the windows at the vast desert plains through which they passed. His eyes had a far-away look in them, and ever and anon he sighed.

Far up the Grand Canyon road late that evening Brady and his three companions still sat watching sadly for the stage which came not. There they had sat in the burning sun without food or water since ten o'clock that morning. They did not speak to each other, but occasionally they cursed, sometimes the birds, sometimes the inanimate things about them. At times they thought of Harrison—but what their thoughts were no one will ever know.

One Touch of Nature

"Pretty good cigar this," remarked the Cowboy.

The Eastern man nodded.

"Nowadays we can buy good ones out where I live, but 'twa'n't very long ago when good cigars were as rare out there as buffaloes are now round Kansas City."

"The enormous increase in population in some of your Western cities is astonishing," remarked the Eastern man.

The Cowboy glanced at him with an amused smile. The Eastern man smiled back good-naturedly.

"What's the joke?" he asked.

"Oh, nothin'," answered the Cowboy, "only I was thinkin' maybe you didn't live out West."

"No, I am a New Yorker," answered the Eastern man.

"Well, I guess they raise pretty good men in both places," remarked the Cowboy.

"Our late war proved that, I think."

The train had stopped, but there were no signs of a station, although two or three rather dilapidated houses and a typical Western saloon could be seen a short distance ahead.

"Wonder what we are stopping here for," remarked the Cowboy; "it strikes me we've been here a pretty long time."

Just then the porter passed the door of the smoking compartment, and the Cowboy called to him:

"Say, porter, what's the matter? Seems to me we have been stoppin' here a whole lot. What's the name of this metropolis?"

"It's mighty lucky you've got whole necks," answered the porter. "The eccentric, or something about the engine, is broke,

Resting His Head on the Cowboy's Knee

and we came mighty near having a bad accident. They've sent on for another engine."

"That's pleasant," remarked the Eastern man. "How long do you think we shall have to stay here before the other engine arrives?"

"Give it up," said the porter. "Maybe an hour, maybe two; can't tell exactly. The train conductor will be along pretty soon and he will know all about it."

"Guess I'll have to appoint myself a committee of one to investigate," remarked the Cowboy.

He arose and went out on the platform of the car, followed by the Eastern man. They climbed down and walked forward to where they saw a crowd gathered about the engine. The eccentric rod had broken short off, and had the engine not been slowing up at the time, the result might have been serious.

The two men strolled down the track for a short distance, and the Cowboy discovered a small colony of prairie dogs. Several of the comical little creatures were sitting on their hind legs on the mounds beside their holes ready to disappear at the least sign of danger. Occasionally one would run from one hole to another a short distance away, usually diving out of sight, to reappear again in a few moments when satisfied that there was no immediate cause for alarm.

The Cowboy amused himself by listlessly throwing small stones at the little animals. After a few moments of this he turned to the Eastern man and said:

"Say, I am goin' to take a little stroll over yonder towards that luxurious mansion and get a drink from the well. Want to go along?"

"With pleasure," answered the Eastern man.

The two strolled slowly towards the house, which was decidedly in need of repair. The fence surrounding it was broken down in many places, weeds and grass filled the little yard in which there were still evidences of some past attempts at ornamentation in the way of flower-beds, and the whole place gave evidence of poverty and lack of care. On the porch was seated a girl apparently between twelve and fourteen years of age. She was hugging an immense shaggy dog and crying as if her heart would break.

"What's the matter, sis?" sympathetically inquired the Cowboy.

"Oh, sir (sob), Jake's goin' to kill my Rover."

"What for?"

The sobs subsided a little and the girl looked up, wiping her eyes on her torn apron.

"Why, he bited Jake because he tried to kiss me and I didn't—want him to—and they are goin' to come and kill him."

"Who is goin' to come and kill him?"

"The feller he bited—Jake."

"There, don't cry, little un; seems to me the purp did the proper caper. What do you think, pardner?"

"In my opinion," answered the Eastern man, "the dog's action was decidedly laudatory."

"And yer think same as I do that the pup hadn't ought to be killed for doin' it?"

"Decidedly not."

"Say, sis, ain't yer got any friends to sort of stand off the feller as allows to do the killin'?"

"No, sir, nobody except father, and he—drinks sometimes and don't care for Rover, and he says he don't want no trouble."

"Ain't yer got no one else?"

"No, sir; nobody but Rover. Mother's dead and I ain't got nobody but Rover. Oh, dear me!"

The girl buried her face in the shaggy coat of her friend and sobbed.

The Cowboy sat down on the step beside her; the dog eyed him inquiringly, but evidently decided he was a friend and wagged his tail slightly.

"Don't cry, my girl; brace up, now; perhaps they won't kill him after all."

"Oh, yes, they will. Jake is over in the saloon now; I saw him go in. He'll do it sure; he hates Rover."

"May I speak to your lap-dog? Will he tear me up much if I pat him?" inquired the Cowboy.

"I wouldn't fool with him, sir; Rover don't like strangers."

The Cowboy snapped his fingers at the dog and called to him: "Come here, Rover."

The splendid animal walked solemnly to him and, resting his head on his knee, looked up steadily into his face.

"Don't seem to be too savage nor nothin'—pretty decent sort of dog."

"Oh, he is, sir; he is just the sweetest, lovingest dog that ever lived. I had him when he wa'n't no bigger than a coon, and couldn't eat nothin' but milk, and he loves me, don't you, Rover? and I love him, and he's all I've got to love in the world, and they're goin' to kill him. Oh, Rover, Rover, what shall I do? what shall I do?"

"Now, sis, tell us about the row—did the dog begin the trouble?"

"Oh, no, sir; Jake came along this morning and I was settin' here playin' with Rover, and Jake he grabbed me and tried to kiss me, and I put up a holler and Rover bited him in the leg. Jake swore and wanted to kill him, but he didn't darst to, and he didn't have no gun; so he's gone home to get his gun and he'll be back pretty quick and he's goin' to kill him."

The girl had stopped crying, but little hysterical sobs choked her from time to time as she talked.

The Cowboy pulled the dog's ears gently and the animal responded by licking his hand.

"Seems to me, pardner, that Jake ain't actin' quite white in this deal."

"It's an outrage," warmly responded the Eastern man.

"I see two fellers," continued the Cowboy, gently stroking the dog's head, "comin' around the corner of the house; maybe we'd better ask 'um please not to hurt the dog."

"I agree with you, most decidedly."

The girl caught sight of the men and uttered a cry of fear. Seizing Rover by the collar, she attempted to drag him inside the house, but the dog braced himself and growled savagely, facing the newcomers.

"Say, pard," remarked the Cowboy quietly, "suppose they are impolite?"

"Well."

"Can you fight?"

"I can try."

"Bully for you, pard; that's the stuff! Shake."

The two men shook hands warmly. Jake and his companion were now very near, and as they came up Jake pulled a large revolver from its holster.

"Now, girl, get away from that dog; I'm goin' to shoot him and I don't want to hurt yer."

The girl turned white, but she placed herself in front of Rover, shielding him as much as she could with her slender body.

"Hold on, my friend," interposed the Cowboy; "you mus'n't shoot that dog."

"Who's goin' to stop me?" sneered Jake.

"I am."

"You are, are you? Well, I'm goin' to shoot him just the same."

"If you shoot that dog I'll give you such a beating yer own mother won't know yer. Sabby?"

"Won't, hey? Perhaps you notice I've got a gun?" said Jake, with an evil look in his eyes.

"I've got one, too, but I ain't pulled it yet," answered the Cowboy slowly.

"See here, now," interposed Jake's companion, "where do I come in? What'll I be doin' all the time when you're smashin' up my pard here?"

"I will try and occupy your attention," quietly said the Eastern man.

"The hell you will!"

"I will."

"Now, gentlemen," said the Cowboy, "we don't want no trouble, but there is a peck of it around here if you fellers try to hurt that dog. The dog bit yer because yer tried to kiss the girl, and he served you damn well right!"

"It's a lie!" interrupted Jake sullenly.

How it was done the Eastern man never knew, but Jake went staggering backward, and when he recovered himself and stood with the blood trickling from a cut under his eye, the Cowboy had him covered with a big Colt's 45, and the eyes which looked at him over the barrel were ugly enough to make a gamer man than Jake feel uneasy.

"Drop yer gun."

Jake dropped it.

"Now move away from it."

Jake did so.

The Cowboy handed his big pistol to the Eastern man and walked straight up to Jake, who looked decidedly uncomfortable.

"Now take it back, or I'll smash yer face," said the Cowboy savagely.

"All right, but, damn you, if it warn't that my leg is sore where the dog bit me I'd fight yer till I couldn't see!"

The Cowboy smiled grimly.

"Good enough! Now get out of here."

"Wait a minute," interposed the Eastern man; "may I make a suggestion?"

"Cert, pard,—why, sure!" answered the Cowboy.

"Well, it seems to me this matter had better be settled amicably if possible; if not, after we are gone something might happen to the dog. After what has happened the gentleman naturally feels an animosity towards the animal. Now, I would suggest that he name a sum of money which he would consider sufficient to compensate him for injuries received. I would be glad to pay a reasonable amount—say ten dollars—in settlement of all damages, if the gentleman will agree not to attempt to injure the dog in any way."

"I'll agree to that," cried Jake eagerly.

"Very well, here is the money." The Eastern man held out a ten-dollar gold piece, which was seized upon by Jake, and without a word he and his companion started in a straight line for the saloon.

The Cowboy shouted after them: "Remember, I'll be back

here next week, and if the dog isn't all right there'll be trouble."
Then, turning to the girl, he said:

"Well, sis, the show's over; the dog's all right, so I guess I'll get
aboard the train. So, so long."

"Please tell me your name, sir, and you, too, sir," turning to
the Eastern man.

"Why, sis, what do you want to know my name for?"

"To pray for you, sir; mother's dead, but I pray every night just
the same, and I ask God to bless Rover—he's all I've got now, you
know. Is that wrong, sir? and to-night and every night I'm goin' to
ask God to bless both o' you for bein' so kind ter Rover and me."

"Oh, that's all right, sis; don't think of it;" the Cowboy's voice
was husky. "Good-by; good-by, Rover, old boy."

He seized the big dog in his arms and turned him over on
his back, holding him down. The dog caught one of the man's
hands in his huge mouth and chewed it gently, while the Cowboy poked him playfully in the ribs with the other. Then the
man jumped up and ran for the car, with Rover leaping and
romping about him, uttering great deep barks of joy. The Eastern man followed more slowly; a cinder or something had got
into his eye, and he was ostentatiously wiping it out with the
corner of his handkerchief.

That night, in the darkness of her room, the girl knelt by the
side of her rough bed, and whispered softly her little prayer:

"God bless mamma, God bless papa, God bless Rover, and
bless the two fellers that was good to me and Rover—I dunno
their names, God, but you do."

The sounds of a slight figure getting into bed were followed by
"'Scuse me, Rover, I didn't mean to step on yer foot; goodnight,
Rover, dear." Several heavy blows on the floor answered her, and
then for a time there was silence. The wind moaned faintly in the
chimney and a rat squeaked and scampered across the floor; then a
board creaked,—the child slept on oblivious to it all,—but at each
new sound the dark form on the floor stirred slightly, a shaggy
head was raised, and wide-open, faithful eyes gazed in the direc-
tion from whence it came, intent, alert, and watchful.

LEONAUR

ALSO FROM LEONAUR
AVAILABLE IN SOFTCOVER OR HARDCOVER WITH DUST JACKET

GARRETT P. SERVISS' SCIENCE FICTION by *Garrett P. Serviss*—Three Interplanetary Adventures including the unauthorised sequel to H. G. Wells' *War of the Worlds--Edison's Conquest of Mars, A Columbus of Space, The Moon Metal.*

JUNK DAY by *Arthur Sellings*—". . . . his finest novel was his last, *Junk Day,* a post-holocaust tale set in the ruins of his native London and peopled with engrossing character types . . . . perhaps grimmer than his previous work but pointedly more energetic." *The Encyclopedia of Science Fiction.*

KIPLING'S SCIENCE FICTION by *Rudyard Kipling*—Science Fiction & Fantasy stories by a Master Storyteller including 'As East As A,B,C' 'With The Night Mail'.

THE COLLECTED SCIENCE FICTION AND FANTASY OF STANLEY G. WEINBAUM: THE BLACK HEART by *Stanley G. Weinbaum*—Classic Strange Tales Including: the Complete Novel The Dark Other, Plus Proteus Island and Others Stories included in this Volume The Dark Other (novel) Proteus Island The Adaptive Ultimate Pymalion's Spectacles.

THE COLLECTED SCIENCE FICTION AND FANTASY OF STANLEY G. WEINBAUM: STRANGE GENIUS by *Stanley G. Weinbaum*—Classic Tales of the Human Mind at Work Including the Complete Novel The New Adam, the 'van Manderpootz' Stories and Others Stories included in this Volume The New Adam (novel) The Brink of Infinity The Circle of Zero Graph The Worlds of If The Ideal The Point of View.

THE COLLECTED SCIENCE FICTION AND FANTASY OF STANLEY G. WEINBAUM OTHER EARTHS by *Stanley G. Weinbaum*—Classic Futuristic Tales Including: Dawn of Flame & its Sequel The Black Flame, plus The Revolution of 1960 & Others.

THE COLLECTED SCIENCE FICTION AND FANTASY OF STANLEY G. WEINBAUM INTERPLANETARY ODYSSEYS by *Stanley G. Weinbaum*—Classic Tales of Interplanetary Adventure Including: A Martian Odyssey, its Sequel Valley of Dreams, the Complete 'Ham' Hammond Stories and Others Stories included in this Volume Mars A Martian Odyssey Valley of Dreams Venus Parasite Planet The Lotus Eaters Uranus The Planet of Doubt Titan Flight on Titan Pluto The Red Peri Io The Mad Moon Europa Redemption Cairn Ganymede Tidal Moon.

SUPERNATURAL BUCHAN by *John Buchan*—Stories of Ancient Spirits, Uncanny Places & Strange Creatures.

ALSO FROM LEONAUR

TROS OF SAMOTHRACE 1: WOLVES OF THE TIBER *by Talbot Mundy*—When his ship is taken and his crew slaughtered Tros of Samothrace is captured by Imperial Rome.

TROS OF SAMOTHRACE 2: DRAGONS OF THE NORTH *by Talbot Mundy*—Tros of Samothrace burns for vengeance and has declared himself the implacable enemy of Rome.

TROS OF SAMOTHRACE 3: SERPENT OF THE WAVES *by Talbot Mundy*—Tros, his allies and the forces of Rome have drawn apart to prepare for the conflict to come.

TROS OF SAMOTHRACE 4: CITY OF THE EAGLES *by Talbot Mundy*—As Tros of Samothrace continues in his attempts to confound Caesar's plans for the invasion of Britain, he journeys to the Eternal City to seek the aid of its great leaders—and Caesar's opponents—Cato, Pompey and the Vestal Virgins themselves!

TROS OF SAMOTHRACE 5: CLEOPATRA *by Talbot Mundy*—Cleopatra—Queen of Egypt—is a formidable character ever ready to play the game of intrigue, betrayal and shifting loyalties to suit her own objectives. Blood will surely be spilt and once again Tros finds himself inexorably caught up in monumental events that threaten his life and those he loves.

TROS OF SAMOTHRACE 6: THE PURPLE PIRATE *by Talbot Mundy*—The epic saga of the ancient world—Tros of Samothrace—draws to a conclusion in this sixth—and final—volume. Julius Caesar has been assassinated and Queen Cleopatra of Egypt finds herself in a perilous position and desperate for allies to secure her power.

THE ILLUSTRATED & COMPLETE BRIGADIER GERARD *by Sir Arthur Conan Doyle*—These are the adventures of Conan Doyle's incomparable French hero-the finest swordsman in the Light Cavalry-Etienne Gerard. Arranged for the first time in historical chronological order, his many enthusiasts can now properly appreciate his colourful career as he fights, loves and blunders his way through the Napoleonic epoch-from his earliest adventure as a young blade determined to reach his lady love despite the unwelcome attention of her fathers bull-through many campaigns and special missions-to the bloody field of Waterloo, the downfall of his beloved Emperor and beyond. This is the complete collection of these classic stories. What makes this edition exceptional is the inclusion of nearly 140 illustrations-mostly by the famed military artist William Barnes Wollen-which accurately portray the spirit of the stories and the uniforms and scenes of the events they portray.

www.ingramcontent.com/pod-product-compliance
Lightning Source LLC
Chambersburg PA
CBHW050309260626
47156CB00005B/1720